*L*ook at me, Susannah," Sister Olive directed. "You must be responsible for keeping Mary safe. Keep her away from that woman so no harm comes to her, so she won't be stolen."

My mouth came open to protest, to say all the things I was thinking, but I looked into Sister Olive's eyes and chose silence.

That night I could not sleep, and so I heard the squeaking of the ladder when Mary climbed into the loft. She crept around the lumpy blanket that was Lydia and squatted beside me. "You should go back to your bed," I whispered, but even as I said it, I reached out and drew her to my side. She snuggled in against me and lay with her head on my arm.

"I want my mam," she said finally.

"I know," I said. "Oh, I know." It was all I knew to say for comfort, but then I thought to stroke her hair, and eventually we both fell asleep.

SUSANNAH

Janet Hickman

SCHOLASTIC INC.
New York Toronto London Auckland Sydney
Mexico City New Delhi Hong Kong Buenos Aires

ISBN 0-439-38112-6

Copyright © 1998 by Janet Hickman.
All rights reserved.
Published by Scholastic Inc., 555 Broadway, New York,
NY 10012, by arrangement with Greenwillow Books, an
imprint of HarperCollins Publishers. SCHOLASTIC
and associated logos are trademarks and/or
registered trademarks of Scholastic Inc.

12 11 10 9 8 7 6 5 4 3 2 1   1 2 3 4 5 6/0

Printed in the U.S.A.   40

First Scholastic printing, November 2001

For SUSANNA and MATT,
for different reasons

O N E

In March of that year, my fourteenth year, a great wind blew down on the settlement at Turtle Creek, littering Sister Olive's garden plot with the limbs of trees. The Elders sent a man to cut the largest branches for firewood, but still there were sticks without number for the littlest girls to gather.

"Be quick," I said as the four of them set to work, for my own hands were already stiff in the cold, bright air. Mary was the only one who looked up at me, her eyes round and sober as always. When the others had scattered to their task, she came to me and plucked at my sleeve.

"Susannah," she said, and her mouth made the hint of a curve, "I saw my mam last night."

"You did not," I told her. Her mother was gone away, and that was the truth. Some of the Sisters had talked of it without knowing I heard them. She had had enough of being a Shaker, so they said, and she had begged for her husband to come away, too, and bring Mary, but of course he would not go himself, nor allow his child to leave. He was strong in the faith, just as my own father was.

"You dreamed again," I said to Mary, trying to be kindly. Yet I thought all at once of my own mother and how she was gone from me forever, and the familiar coils of hurt inside me sprang up into my throat so that I had to swallow against them. "You dreamed," I repeated, "just like those other times."

"No," she said, and her tiny, sharp chin took on a stubborn tilt. "I saw her."

I wanted to scoop her up then, tell her that her mam surely did long to be with her, but I thought I dare not. Like us all, she would need to learn to do without mother or father, either one. God was parent enough, one of the Elders had said to me. It was such a hard thing that I sometimes wept when I thought of it.

My distress must have been plain in my face, for Mary caught my hand and squeezed it. "When I carry the bucket for water," she whispered, "my mam is there. When it is almost dark, in the woodlot."

"There are shadows at dusk," I said. "Sometimes

little girls see what is not there."

She smiled at me forgivingly, as if I were the young one who did not understand, and went off silently to gather her share of sticks.

Foolishness, I said to myself, but I resolved to watch the woodlot, not because I hoped to raise an alarm but because I hoped to see a mother with her child.

⚜

My own mother was a special creature, full of songs and stories. She was "accomplished." That was the word my father used in answer to a churchman who asked how it was that I, a girl from so lonely and wild a place as Kentucky, could read and write and figure. My mother taught me, of course, just as she taught me to bake bread and tend a garden and think for myself. She was a well-schooled woman from Virginia, where her family had a fine house near the James River. I was born in that house and had to be kept from tumbling down its broad staircase as I learned to walk. Sometimes I thought I could almost remember that place and the tall grandmother who held me, but more likely it was my mother's stories of them that I recalled. Her eyes were like two suns when she talked of home, and I warmed myself many a cold evening in their light.

My mother must have loved my father very much to trade Virginia for Kentucky. Our house at Cane Ridge was almost as plain as the poorest cabin on the farthest hill; my father's business dealings brought little profit. I know that he loved my mother, although he was such a stern man and so dour of expression that it was hard to tell. Still, it was after she . . . died . . . that he felt the spirit and began to go to all the preachings for miles and miles around. Then he heard about the Shakers, and nothing would do but that he come north of the Ohio to join the new gathering at Turtle Creek. And I, being but thirteen years at the time, must come with him.

My father seemed to be much pleased with what he found in Ohio. Missionaries from the Shakers of New England had come to the New Light Presbyterian Church at Turtle Creek some five years before, the Elders said. Since that time they had persuaded most of the congregation as well as a good number of others to become Believers, for that was what the Shakers called themselves.

When my father and I came to the place, there was little to see but a scatter of buildings where two roads crossed, an expanse of flat land cleared for farming, and a great hustle of work: soap-making, wood-chopping, harvesting of corn. But the Elders told us Turtle Creek would soon grow into a village with the new converts that were coming every week.

It would be like the Shaker towns in the East, they said. There would be proper housing for everyone so that Believers could live together, not here and there in houses throughout the countryside, waiting for a place. There would be an increase of prosperous fields, they said, so that no one would want for food. And there would be orderly ways of work and worship, which would bring peace to my father's spirit.

He nodded as they talked to him that day, and I could see how his eyes took in the size of the barns and the Meeting House, which were as large as any structures we had seen since we had set out north and east from the town of Cincinnati. The Elders pointed out to him where the flax and broomcorn grew, in season, and they spoke of their mill and horses and the fine milk cows they had and how he would share in all that by sharing in their beliefs.

I did not learn all I should have that day because I fell to puzzling over the doors I saw. There were two just alike in one wall of the Meeting House and two more, just alike, for the house where the Elders said they lived with the most steadfast of the faithful. I could see that only men went in and out one of the doors; only women used the other. It was odd, I thought. The house itself was large and entirely plain, and I felt somehow that my mother would have found no comfort in it.

Still, everything seemed to suit my father. He could barely wait until the next day, the Sabbath, to declare himself to the Shakers. We went as visitors to their Meeting, which was so crowded that I could scarcely tell who were the Believers and who had come in from the country around about to gape or scoff. Then after the singing and the preaching the Shakers got up and danced, women on one side of the room, men on the other, stomping and swaying until some of them cried out and fell in a heap among the others. It frightened me so that my hands shook, and I wanted my father to take me far away from Turtle Creek forever. But he watched all the goings-on with a glow on his face such as I had never seen there. After Meeting he pulled me along, though I mumbled in protest, as he sought out the Elders.

"I pray that you will have me, a sinful man, in this godly community," he said to them. "I beg to be allowed to join you." He frowned as if he had forgotten something and nudged me forward. "My daughter and I both beg to join you."

"I do not," I said from my heart, but my words did not matter. By law a father has the right to control his children, to say what they must do and where they must go. Kind men take their children's wishes into account, and that was what I had expected of my father. But whatever I said that day, he did not seem to hear it, nor did any of the others. And that was how I came to live among the Shakers.

From the beginning I was sent to live in the little house of Sister Olive Gatwood, a widow whose job it was to take in children of families new to the Believers, at least until room was made for them in the new Children's Family—a special house just for the young. Sister Olive's household had only girls, for boys were sent then to Brother Aaron Woods across the way. Male and female were always to be separate, according to the Shaker way of believing. Men and women would live in the same house, Sister Olive told me, but they could have no contact with one another except when there was careful supervision, at meals or at worship. Proper Shaker buildings had two entrances and two stairways, she said, so that the Brothers and Sisters could keep themselves pure, never touching people of the opposite sex even by accident.

The cruel surprise was not so much that boys and girls were to be separate as it was finding that children must live always apart from their parents. I knew why the little girls cried at night, sometimes, long after they should have grown accustomed to the lumpy pallets where they slept. How were any of us to understand why it was wrong for families to be together? If we were all to turn our hearts to God, so be it. But why were we denied the company of those we already knew and held dear? I could only imagine what my mother would have said.

Mary was the newest child and almost the youngest, not six years old. Yet she was the one who seldom cried. Just once, on her first night among us, had I seen her cheeks wet. I gathered her up into my lap then and rocked back and forth on the bench beside the fireplace, not caring if Sister Olive rebuked me. Olive must have been an eager convert. Everywhere she looked she found nothing but rules; one would have thought they were written on her spectacles. Many a time before then she had predicted damnation for big girls like me, girls with undisciplined hearts and independent ways. But Sister Olive had snored all the while I was rocking with Mary and tucking her in, adding her to the row that slept huddled together in the far corner: round little Celia; Elizabeth, who always coughed; silent Betsy; and now Mary. The next morning Mary told me that her mother had visited her, had whispered her name through the cracks in the wall.

"You dreamed, Mary," I said to her then.

I thought much about Mary's dreams that bitter day after the big wind. It came to me strongly that she should have a mother. I had no hopes for myself, except for the reunion in heaven that my father had mentioned so often in his prayers as we traveled to Ohio. But I could have hope for Mary. When the weary day was over, I took that thought up into the loft with me, into the warmth of my blanket. If Mary's mother did come now and again for a glimpse of her, I could perhaps—Sleep came to stop my thoughts and plans, although in truth I had no plan. I did not know what I could do.

In April of that year, my fourteenth year, the year 18 and 10, Mr. Benjamin Gatwood walked out from the town of Lebanon to visit his brother's widow, Olive. So he told me when I opened the door to him. Then he looked straight past my ear.

"Dearest Olive," he said with no further greeting, "I beseech you to come to your senses!" He had a wheezy voice, rather high.

"You!" Sister Olive grabbed her stirring spoon and whacked the side of the kettle over the fire. It wobbled so that some of our precious soup spilled out. I stood with my mouth agape, but Mr. Gatwood smiled.

"Ill temper is unbecoming to a woman," he said, as if he had gained an advantage that pleased him much.

Sister Olive took a breath and settled her heavy features into their usual scowl.

"I bid you the Lord's welcome," she said, her

voice belying her words. Then she turned to me. "Susannah, go look to the little girls. See they've done their chores, and then take them to hunt for greens in the ditch by the woodlot. And step along!"

I nodded and slipped past our visitor as demurely as I could. But once I was out in the air, I had to laugh. I had never seen Sister Olive's face so red. I thought I might better have stayed inside to protect Mr. Gatwood from her mighty spoon. She always puffed up like a sick toad when her husband's kinfolk came to fuss with her about giving the Gatwood land to the Shakers. Her late husband had promised that each of his nephews would have a few acres, so they all said, but now that Olive had offered all his worldly possessions to the Believers, the nephews would get nothing. Sister Olive said they should be satisfied that the land would give its yield to the godly, and they should leave her alone.

I had seen quite a number of Gatwoods come to call on Sister Olive, and I thought every one to be unpleasant, though not all in the same way. Still, I understood their complaint. Had not my own father given the Elders my mother's silver teapot to buy feed for Shaker horses? Had he not made them a gift of the sparkling comb she once wore in her hair, the comb I thought one day to wear in mine? My hand reached up of its own accord to touch the thick brown curls that would have held that comb.

Instead my fingers found the plain little white cap we all wore, a square bonnetlike affair without strings. An ugly thing. My laughter bubbled away. I had no need of a comb with my hair in such a prison.

I took a breath. "Mary!" I shouted. "Elizabeth! Girls!" There was a rustling behind the shed, and I ran that way. "I spy you!" I called, though I had only guessed. "Come out!"

"I don't care if you spy me or not," a gruff voice said, and I took a step back as a boy some taller than I came walking through the bushes at the corner of the shed. Boys were not welcome at Sister Olive's.

"Are you just come to the Shakers?" I asked, for newcomers did sometimes lose their way. He laughed then, and I recognized the Gatwood chin.

"I am not so ignorant as to get caught in all of this," he said. Right there in the dooryard he hooted and shuffled his feet in imitation of the dancing we all must do at Meeting. I still thought the dancing was odd myself, but I had learned to take peculiar pleasure from it. I had no wish to join his mocking.

"Why are you skulking here?" I demanded.

For a moment he looked at me as if I were too low among God's creations to deserve an answer. Then he sniffed. "I'm just waiting out here while my grandfather warns dear old Olive about all the trouble that's coming."

"What trouble?" One or two small worms of

worry moved inside me. Some time before, a new barn had been set ablaze in the night; the Elders spoke of it as the work of enemies among the world's people, a trial for the Believers. "What trouble?" I said again, more insistently.

"Nothing much. Folks don't like what might go on here. Shaker ways aren't natural, that's what they say in town. I hear some folks might chase all the old Shakers back where they came from, that's all, unless you people begin to get the hint on your own. So it isn't good for Olive to be mixed in with it."

"I don't believe you," I said to him as the little girls came running like chicks to a hen. "You are only telling a tale." But I believed enough to make my heart thump, both then and many times after.

T W O

*T*hat spring a coughing sickness came to Sister Olive's household. All the small girls took it, as well as Jane and Abby, the middle ones. As for Lydia, the girl nearest my age, she coughed only a little although she complained a lot. It was Lydia's nature to whine; she had been a long time with Sister Olive and had more interest in holiness than in my friendship, a circumstance for which I often gave silent thanks. Sister Olive herself was laid low for two days. She asked me then where I had learned to be such a good nurse, for I nursed them all, but I did not find the words to tell her.

Mary was the first of the little girls to recover, and then she had a setback that left her pale as water.

For a week she called out in the night for her mother, pitiable to hear but very wearisome. In the day she tagged along behind Sister Olive or Lydia or me, clinging to our skirts. "Keep that child out of the way!" Olive would say to me when Mary got too near the fire and "Make that child be quiet!" when she sniffled through the prayers at mealtime.

On one of those days, when the trees were just greening, Sister Olive sent me on the long walk to the Elders' Family for medicines. I was to tell Eldress Ruth that we had need of something more to quiet the little ones' coughing at night, for their fussing kept us all from sleep. My mother would have reached into the chimney corner, I thought, and drawn out a pinch of this herb or that, and everyone would have been breathing clear before the next Sabbath. But now her medicine packets were empty and far away, hanging limp beside the window where I left them. Or carried away by the great cat that screeched so shrill in the woods behind our little house in Kentucky.

"Susannah!" Sister Olive's sharp tone brought me to myself and I thought ruefully that she was my great cat in Ohio. "Did you hear me? Take Mary," she said. I sighed and nodded. I meant to take her, anyway, to save her from Olive's yammering.

Right away the little one came to me with her arms up, wanting to be carried.

"You are too big for that." I scoffed for Olive's ears, but I set Mary on my hip the moment we were out of sight. She was scrawny as a bird, lighter by far than wet laundry or iron kettles. Besides, I thought to warm her from the afternoon's lingering chill. The sun was a tease that day, peeking now and then through a tumble of clouds.

"Shall I sing to you?" I said when she shivered, but she shook her dark little head against my chest. Mary was a winsome child, I thought, but not an easy one. I realized all at once how my arms ached from stretching around her. When I set her on a stump to rest myself, she slid down onto the rutted path and walked ahead, finding violets in places where I would not have thought to look.

I could hear the bustle of the Elders' Family lot before their dwelling house came to sight through the trees. My chest grew tight. Coming to the heart of the Shaker settlement always made me feel so, although I did not know why. The Elders and Eldresses lived here, and all of those who were called Old Believers, the easterners who had lived long in the faith and had come from the state of New York to make proper Shakers of us in the West. The Brothers lived in one side of the space, the Sisters in the other, just as Olive had told me, with separate doors so they might stay always a godly distance apart. They thought we had much to learn, and they spoke often at Meeting to tell us so. We should not eat so much pork, they said; pork was bad for the stomach. We should not talk while we worked, they said; silence would bring us closer to God. And on, and on. I could not think of anything for which the Old Believers did not have a rule.

Eldress Ruth was in the dooryard that day surrounded by other women; I saw they were visitors by their shawls and the drape of their skirts.

"Please, Sister," I said to the nearest of the Believers, "I was sent to talk to Eldress Ruth." I held both of Mary's hands to keep her from rubbing her sleeve across her nose.

"She has a great heap of work to do," the Sister said. I had seen this woman at Meeting; she was one of those who spoke in tongues when the dancing grew most frenzied, shouting words none of us had ever heard. But her voice was ordinary now. "There are twenty come for supper," she said.

It would have been best to lower my eyes, for I had learned that humility was a trait much valued by the Believers. Instead, I shook my head and raised my chin the way my mother had always done when she thought her business was important.

"Sister Olive Gatwood sent me," I said clearly. "The little girls cough all night for want of medicine." Mary hid her face in my apron. "Sister Olive has not been well herself."

The woman took stock of me and beckoned to Eldress Ruth, and so we had our moment with her. In spite of myself, I liked her kindly face. She spoke to us as if we were real kin to her, and she invited us to stand inside while she selected the very herbs my mother would have chosen to fill my apron pockets. She did not seem to mind that we stared, Mary and I, at the bare perfection of the little sitting room where she had led us; I had never seen a room scrubbed so clean or left quite so tidy.

When I turned to leave, Eldress Ruth patted my shoulder. "Remind Sister Olive that you are growing," she said. "You will need something new to wear." I felt my cheeks flame as I nodded and tugged Mary away.

All the Old Believers and their most trusted converts wore clothing made to the same pattern, as we were all to do when there was cloth enough and time enough for the sewing. New girls could expect Shaker outfits by the time their dresses from home were too worn or too tight. I dreaded the thought of the high neckline without so much as one tuck for ornament and the tight sleeves and the dark petticoats that were in store for me. I pulled at the green checked bodice I wore, the one my mother had helped me to trim with row after row of green braid. Touching it made me feel close to her, helped me remember how her fingers flew and how her needle clicked against the silver thimble her own mother had bequeathed to her. I wanted to wear my green checked bodice forever.

I wished then that I could fly away, wished that I could take wing and be free. At the very least I wanted to pluck Mary up and skim over the path toward the Gatwood house, where I could hide myself in some familiar task. I would pretend that I was still at home in Kentucky, still had hopes of being a notable housewife one day with a husband and babies and—

"Susannah!" Mary's cry interrupted my thoughts. "Look!" she said. She set her heels in the soft earth and would go no farther. We had just come to the Elders' barn, and Mary's eyes glittered with desire. She was a child much taken with animals, always chattering at squirrels and rabbits. She had doted on the chickens and the milk cow that had lived until lately in a ramshackle barn at Sister Olive's. But horses were Mary's favorite; she hoped every day to see one.

I looked with her at the wide, silent doorway. "I'm sorry, Mary," I said. "All the horses will be at work now. The men will have taken them out to the fields to plow, I think."

"But we could look," she said in her whispery little voice worn from coughing. "Please?"

"You look," I said, for I couldn't deny her. "Go

quick," I said, knowing that the barn was many times bigger than Sister Olive's house. "And be careful." I did not want her to run afoul of any of the Brothers at some chore.

I fidgeted on the path with the wind tugging my skirts while Mary went looking, and I was glad for her quick return. But her face was silent and troubled, and the farther we walked, the more guilt I felt for allowing her such a disappointment.

"Shall I tell you a story?" I offered.

"No," she said. "Don't."

We had almost reached the woodlot when Mary stopped and faced me. "Why was that horse sleeping?" she demanded. I could not tell what the feeling was that showed in her face. "Why was he sleeping so strange?"

"What horse?" I felt a drop of rain on the back of my hand. "Hurry along," I said, reaching toward her.

"The one in the barn!" Her thin voice grew louder. "He didn't move at all!"

"All creatures sleep," I said, but I did not believe that she had seen a horse, or any other animal. Mary could be a nuisance sometimes, building stories in her head and telling them for true. Once she had almost convinced me that Sister Olive had found a bear cub and was keeping it in the wash kettle.

"He didn't move," Mary repeated. "And his

mouth was open like this." She stretched her own mouth wide and let her tongue hang at an odd angle. I flinched in spite of myself.

"Don't make your face so ugly," I said in a voice as sharp as Sister Olive's. "And don't tell such stories, either. If Mrs. Gatwood hears you, she'll preach your ears off."

"No!" Mary wailed. "There was too a horse!" Each of her cheeks showed a tinge of pink. I had never seen her in such a temper. "It didn't look right!" Her voice pitched up toward a scream. "It looked bad!" She closed her hands into hard little fists and began flailing at me.

"Stop!" I screeched. "Stop it, you wicked girl!"

As soon as the word was out of my mouth, I regretted it, but she did stop. And then I saw that Mary was no longer paying any attention to me. She stood with wet cheeks and trembling arms, transfixed by something behind me. Her lips formed a single soundless word—*Mam*—and I whirled in time for just one glimpse of a moss brown cloak and dark hair streaming free.

"Wait!" I called. "Stop! I did not mean—" But in an instant the slender figure was gone among the trees, and rain came pouring upon us. I snatched Mary up and held her close.

"You are not a wicked girl," I said into her ear. "You are not."

That night my own forehead burned with fever, my chest felt bound with an iron band, my limbs could not stand the weight of a cover. Too weak to climb to my place in the loft, I lay for three days on a pallet near Sister Olive's bedstead. I believe that I was sick unto death and that one night someone was sent to fetch my father. In my delirium my mind came again and again to my mother, but it was my father's face that I saw—a sorrowing, puzzled face.

"I should have sent you to Margaret," he said, or he seemed to say it, for the words were plain in my ear. Then he prayed for me in such tormented tones that the little girls woke and cried, and I think I slipped off to sleep just to escape the din of it. Or perhaps that part was a dream, for when I was better, no one mentioned my father's visit at all.

THREE

After we came to the Shakers, my father stayed in a house some distance from Gatwoods' with other newcomers. The only time I could hope to see him was at Meeting. *See* is the best word; he had many kindly looks for me but never a thing to say. When my illness subsided, I was determined I should speak to him and he to me. Although my hands were not quite steady that first Sunday after I was up and about, I sped through my morning chores so that I could take special care in getting ready for Meeting. I arranged my apron and neckerchief to cover much of my gown, one that had been my mother's. It was not quite plain enough to be altogether acceptable, but neither was it tight enough to embarrass me. I did not wish

Eldress Ruth to take special notice of me on this day when I felt I must talk to my father.

All my hurry and fuss made me cough so much that Sister Olive said I need not go to Meeting if I did not feel well enough. Our Saturday service with the little girls would keep my heart on the right course for one more week, she said, and I could stay behind and help Jane look after them.

"I would not like to miss another Meeting, Sister," I told her. It was not quite a lie.

"Best go on then." Sister Olive was pleased by my determination, I could tell. She called each of us in turn—Abby, Lydia, and me—to stand by her and tell how we had prepared our thoughts for worship. What I mumbled then I do not know, for I had prepared nothing except questions for my father. Did you really speak to me of a Margaret? I would ask him, for I knew no one named Margaret. Why might I have gone to her? I tried to imagine this faceless woman. I knew nothing of her, yet the very possibility of her connection to me was such a hopeful thing that I scarcely dared consider it.

My thoughts so occupied me that I took little notice of the brightness of the day as we set off toward the Meeting House.

"There will be a great crowd of the world's people at this day's Meeting," Lydia whispered, and I nodded, paying little attention.

"Do you remember the first fair day last spring?" she went on. "The time when so many visitors gathered that two big women tried to sit in the same spot on the bench and fell out on the floor during the dancing?"

"I was not here," I reminded her, although Lydia had described the scene so many times that I felt I had witnessed it. I was in Kentucky then, I thought, when the leaves were the size of a squirrel's ear and my mother planted seeds to make flowers that I could not stay to see. I sighed, and such a fit of coughing took me that my legs felt weak and my eyes streamed tears. I had to stop to get my breath.

"Don't be slow, Susannah. You will make us late." Lydia peered ahead of us, where Abby and Sister Olive were almost out of sight. I had no wish to be late, for it was only in the odd moments before Meeting, or after, that there might come an opportunity to speak to my father.

"You are sorry, I should think, for missing the last Meeting," Lydia said, not slowing her pace to wait for me. It was hard for me to hear her, what with the noise of birds around us and the clatter of wagons and horses ahead, where the crowd of Sunday visitors was gathering.

"I have never been so taken with the Spirit," Lydia said. "I don't know how long I was in a swoon after I labored at the dance."

I dipped my head lest she should turn around and catch me smiling. Lydia had a way of keeping track of her swoons after she had them; had I a blossom for each report, I would have had a whole field of flowers.

"We all rose up out of the depths of despair into the light," Lydia said. I nearly failed to make the effort to listen to her then, because she had slipped into her most holy, most tiresome voice. "There was such sorrow," she went on, "and such indignation when the Elder spoke of the latest evil done to us by the world's people, and then—"

"Wait," I said, trying to lengthen my steps. "What evil do you mean?"

She halted long enough to turn and show me a smug face. "Oh, of course, you didn't hear. The wicked ones poisoned one of the Elders' horses. And they were brazen enough to do it right within the barn."

I would not have shuddered any harder had I stepped upon a snake. "But why?" I protested, thinking first of the blameless horse. And then, realizing that little Mary had seen the poor lifeless thing, I sucked in a ragged breath that sent me again into spasms of coughing.

"Go back to the house, Susannah!" Abby called to me from far ahead. "Sister Olive says you are not fit for Meeting."

"'Go back,' she said," Lydia repeated. "And don't worry. I'll tell you all about everything if I get time." She twitched her skirt and hurried toward the others.

I was alone then on the narrow track from the Gatwood house, struggling to quiet my cough and to still my racing thoughts. I would not get to see my father. If only I could speak to him, I thought, I would beg him to send me from this place. Perhaps there was no such person as Margaret. It would not matter. I would rather be bound out as a tavern girl than to be here. If my mother were alive, surely she would not have me stay in a place that had been a target for flames and for poison. Nor would she want me in a place that did not honor the natural bonds of family. And just as I thought that, a hand took my wrist and pulled me quickly into the shelter of the trees.

I tried to cry out, but no breath came. All I could do was stare at the woman who held me in her grasp.

"Girl," she whispered, "how is my baby? Is my baby well?" Even in my fright I knew the eyes, clear blue circles rimmed with the thinnest tracing of black.

I barely breathed. "Is it Mary that you mean? Are you Mary's mother?"

She nodded, tightening her fingers on my wrist.

"I have seen you with her. You must tell me how she fares."

"She—she had a sickness in her chest," I stammered, "but she is better now."

"Ohh." The woman let her hand relax and fall away from mine; something soft flashed across her face and was gone again. "Thanks be," she said, and smoothed one long dark wing of hair away from her cheek. I wondered what sort of woman she was to let her hair swing free on the Lord's Day—no coil or plait or comb, not even a poor ribbon.

I think I was not yet really well that day. My eyes tricked me, showed me my own mother's hair, lying loose against her pillow with no hand to brush it but mine. I began suddenly to cry as a little child cries, chest heaving.

Mary's mother drew back from me. "What ails you, girl?" And then, when I could not answer, she came closer and placed a gentle hand on each of my shoulders. "What have they done to you here? What of your family?"

I fought against the coughing fit that threatened me; I drew away from the warm touch that was not rightfully mine. "I am William Arden's daughter," I said finally. "My name is Susannah." I made myself stand straighter and remember the manners my mother had taught me. "I beg pardon for such an outburst," I said, clearing my throat. "I have had

some illness of my own, and I am not quite myself."
She studied me, fixed her eyes so intently on my face
that I had to look down at my skirt. "Besides," I said,
"sometimes I miss . . . my home."

"Of course," she said. "Of course you do." Her
voice softened. "Susannah," she said, "perhaps you
can imagine how I miss my little Mary. And I worry.
Please promise me that you will take care of her.
Please."

"There's always someone watching over the little
ones," I said. "And there has been plenty to eat."

Mary's mother shook her head. "That is not what
I mean." She raised one hand to her throat and
began to fidget with her collar. "Trouble will come
here. Ugliness and danger. I pray that you will keep
my Mary safe."

"What danger?"

"I cannot stay here," she said, edging off among
the trees.

"How do you know of this trouble?" I pressed her.

"That is no matter," she said. "But you can be
sure of it. So please promise me. Please remember."

"Perhaps I will be gone," I said boldly, but my
knees had begun to tremble. I do not think she heard
me, anyway, for she had turned and begun her swift
escape into the woods.

"Why should I stay here and wait for trouble?"
I said aloud to the green lace on the trees, to the

squirrel on the path, to the bits of spring sky that showed above me. "Why should I be the one to look after Mary? Why should I be in this place at all?" I expected no answer, and true to my expectation, no answer came. No voice sounded from a cloud, no word appeared written on the earth before me. All that was sent me that day in the way of a sign was Mary herself, who saw me coming back to the Gatwood house and ran to walk with me, holding tight to my hand. So disturbed was I that I could not bring myself to tell her of my encounter. Instead, I willed myself to think of the name Margaret, of the promise attached to that word. Yet when I tried to make an image in my mind, the face that came— blue eyes, black hair, firm chin—was the face of Mary's mam.

FOUR

*T*t was in May of that year, when the little apple tree in Sister Olive's dooryard bloomed, that I first thought how odd it was for spring always to come right on, soft and new and beautiful, in spite of everything. My mother had loved the spring, had exclaimed over the sorriest little green shoots, had held her breath so as not to disturb a nesting thrush. If she had been put to the test of the rumors that came to Turtle Creek that spring, she would have drawn serenity from the season. Or so I thought, and the thought calmed me, even when an entire wagonload of Gatwoods appeared in Sister Olive's dooryard.

Lydia and I were working in the garden plot when they came, and since they called Sister out to them and shouted at her, we did not miss a word.

"Dear Olive," Mr. Benjamin Gatwood intoned from his wagon seat, "I advise you as a brother to give up this life at once."

Seated beside him was a plump woman that I took for his wife. "Send these youngsters back to their parents," she said sweetly, as if that would be an easy thing, simply done. I pressed the earth far too firm across the tiny seeds in my row. "You can come live with us then, Olive," the woman went on, and I thought with some surprise that her voice rang true.

Sister Olive kept shaking her head. "No," she said. "Mayhap you mean well, Eunice, but I have found the path to heaven, and I do not mean to stray from it now." Beside me Lydia's face glowed approval. In the back of the wagon three boys—the one I had seen before and two that were smaller—exchanged rude laughter.

"You should take the godly way, too, Eunice," Sister Olive went on. "It is not too late. Put the pleasures of the flesh behind you. Give up your husband and live pure, the Shaker way."

Poor Eunice Gatwood! There came such a flush across her face that the folds of her white neckscarf turned to pink.

"Enough!" Mr. Gatwood rose to his feet right smartly, I thought, for a man of his years. "You have lost all sense of shame to speak such words in front of these grandsons of ours!" He glanced over his shoulder at the young Gatwoods, who were covering their laughter with their hands. He did not seem to see Lydia and me, although the boys looked at us through their fingers. I heard Lydia catch her breath across the row from me.

"Right in the Holy Book, dear Olive, it says that a man shall cleave to his wife, and—"

"Stop!" Mrs. Gatwood pulled at her husband's coat. "You needn't fuss and argue, Mr. Gatwood. Leave it to the preachers. Just tell the news we came to tell, and we'll be on our way."

Sister Olive scowled. "I have no need of the world's news," she said, and she pointed her lumpy forefinger at the occupants of the wagon. "The only good news comes from the Almighty, and the only word I trust comes from the Believers. I'm the one should be telling you the news. Have you heard about Christ's Second Appearing?"

I bit my lip. I wanted to hear the Gatwoods' message, whatever it was. I had no taste for another lesson about the Second Appearing—about Mother Ann, the founder of the Shakers, and how the Believers thought her to be a second Christ, the Holy One in female form. In truth it was an idea that appealed to me, for why should it not be so that the Spirit lived in woman as well as man? What was my own mother, after all, but a little of God on earth? Yet when Olive prattled on about it, it seemed an unlikely thing somehow.

"Have you heard about Mother Ann?" Olive went on, her voice rising.

"Blasphemy!" shouted Benjamin Gatwood. "Say no more!"

"Peace!" cried his wife. "Peace, both of you!" And then the boys stood up in the wagon bed and it was hard to tell who was shouting what. For a moment I thought the horses would bolt and send Gatwoods flying across the bare garden. And then Lydia began to weep so violently that I feared she would swoon right into the bean rows.

For my part, I tried to think what my mother would have done, but it was hard to imagine that she would ever have encountered such a scene. In the midst of the commotion the door of the house swung open, and three of the little girls spilled out, bawling.

"Go back, children!" Sister Olive said at once, and two of them turned and fled. Mary, who was the third, darted around the corner of the wagon and came straight to me. I stood and gathered her into my skirt.

"It's all right," I whispered. "It's only noise."

But it was suddenly quiet. Lydia had composed herself, and all the Gatwoods had turned to stare at Mary.

"It's Sarah Bay's child," Mrs. Gatwood said finally.

"Thomas Bay's little girl," her husband said.

The tall boy smiled down over the side of the wagon. "It's Mary," he said. "Hello, Mary."

"Don't be forward, Joseph," the woman said. "And sit down, boys, all of you." Mary wrapped her fists in my skirt and did not look around.

Eunice Gatwood glanced from Sister Olive to Mary and me and back again. "Mrs. Bay is suffering mightily," she said softly. "She grieves about this separation from her daughter."

"The woman is naught but a troublemaker," Olive said.

I rubbed Mary's head with both my hands, thinking to stop her ears. But I might have known better; her little body was stiff with listening.

Mr. Gatwood settled himself on the wagon bench and adjusted the reins in his hands. "She might be a perfect woman, dear Olive, if Tom Bay would go back to his home and put his family together again."

Sister Olive snorted. "She had a chance to turn her heart to heaven, same as her husband, but she fell back into the world." Olive turned her eyes to me as she spoke. "She lurks around here still, some say, hoping to snatch up this child. Or worse. I say, 'Be done with her.'"

I set my face so that no one could see inside me.

"Best you not be done with her quite so soon," Mrs. Gatwood said. "It's Mrs. Bay's news that we came here to give you."

"People speak more and more now of harm against the Shakers," her husband said, and his voice took on an urgency I had not heard before. "Colonel Smith—the one whose son is here—is planning some violent act, we think. He says the Shakers are holding his grandchildren against their mother's will, and he is determined to get them away from here, home to their mother."

I caught my breath. I did not know who the Smith children were, but I thought they were lucky to have someone who would speak for them and for their mother.

"Colonel Smith is a man of action, Olive," Mr. Gatwood went on. "He has much support in the town and in the countryside. Mrs. Bay can list out two dozen names or more."

My fingers tightened on Mary's shoulder, and I saw Sister Olive frown. Then her face relaxed.

"The Bay woman told you this?" Olive shook her head. "Such a lie was not worth your trip." Then she called to me. "Come, Susannah, and bring Mary into the house. Lydia can finish there. And good day to all of you," she said, dismissing the Gatwoods.

Lydia fell to work, blushing, since Joseph Gatwood

gawked at her all the while his grandfather was turning the wagon under the apple tree. I took my time with Mary, talking soft and slow to her that I might calm myself, and so I was there to raise my hand in a neighborly gesture to Eunice Gatwood as the wagon went by. The news had left me uneasy, no doubt of that, for any threat of violence made me fret. But my fear had the company of so many other feelings that I did not know which would govern me from one moment to the next.

Later, in the dim light of the house, Sister Olive drew me away from Mary and made my orders clear.

"Do you know what that Bay woman looks like? She has hair as black as a crow and the same eyes as Mary. And there's not one trustworthy bone in her body. If you see her," Sister Olive said, "stay far away from her. Say not one word to her. Do you understand?"

I nodded, eyes down.

"Look at me, Susannah," Sister Olive directed. "You must be responsible for keeping Mary safe. Keep her away from that woman so no harm comes to her, so she won't be stolen."

My mouth came open to protest, to say all the things I was thinking, but I looked into Sister Olive's eyes and chose silence.

That night I could not sleep, and so I heard the

squeaking of the ladder when Mary climbed into the loft. She crept around the lumpy blanket that was Lydia and squatted beside me. "You should go back to your bed," I whispered, but even as I said it, I reached out and drew her to my side. She snuggled in against me and lay with her head on my arm.

"I want my mam," she said finally.

"I know," I said. "Oh, I know." It was all I knew to say for comfort, but then I thought to stroke her hair, and eventually we both fell asleep.

FIVE

ere is how the time passed in the spring of that year: like turtles inching in the sun, like old molasses on the lip of a jug, slower than slow. I wondered if we might all be poisoned like the Elders' horse or cut down as we tended the garden, but Sister Olive kept us at our regular tasks. Mary grew more silent as the days went on, her round eyes watchful. I in turn watched Mary, having been charged twice to keep her safe, although I could not be sure from what threat I needed to protect her. During that time I did not once see Mary's mam, although I often took the chores that would give me reason to go out among the outbuildings and to the edge of the woods that I might look for her.

If there was any change in Olive Gatwood, it was that she began to take special pains with our spiritual education. Twice in the week we must confess our sins, for Mother Ann had taught that confession was cleansing to the soul. All of the older converts were required to confess one to another from their hearts every week, Sister Olive assured us. Abby and Jane and I, and Lydia, worked and worried at this exercise once midweek as well as each Sabbath after the midday meal, while the little girls were having exhortations from Sister Olive. The Sabbath was the day when I felt always most troubled, having just had sight of my father at Meeting but— again and again—no chance for words with him. Nor was I eager to bare my soul to any other. My mother had taught me that in her religion, which I felt was also mine, sorrow for one's transgressions was spoken directly to God; it was only the Roman Church that required an intermediary. Among the Presbyterians and the Baptists and even the New Lights my father had taken me to see, every preacher had demanded that we confess our sinful nature, but they seemed to mean all at once, as a way to salvation, not twice a week, as a ritual. No wonder that in the crowds of visitors who came to Meeting there were always a few who stood outside and shouted that Shakers were nothing but followers of the pope in disguise.

I know I was daydreaming that Sabbath, the one following the Gatwoods' visit, thinking back to my Sundays in Kentucky. We would go to services, my mother and father and I, and afterward my father would doze in his chair, pretending to read Scripture. Then my mother and I would whisper together about the day's sermon and sing the hymns she knew and laugh quietly at our wrong notes. That was far more cleansing to my spirit than sitting knee to knee with Lydia, practicing the confession I would report to Sister Olive before our supper.

"You cannot be so silent," Lydia urged me that day, although Sister Olive had told us each to be quiet as the other gathered her thoughts. "Surely you are no work of perfection, Susannah. There must be something that weighs on your soul."

I scowled at her. "There is much that weighs on my heart," I said. I should have let my tongue stop there, but with that one part of my mind back in Kentucky, my words came on unchecked. "Mary Bay troubles my heart," I said. "Mary and her mother. I confess my disbelief that God means for the Shakers to keep little children away from their parents."

Lydia sucked in her breath at this display of blasphemy, but I went right on. "Mary wants her mam, and Mrs. Bay wants Mary, and I can't see why Mary's father should make her stay here. When does he even see her? What does he know of her?"

"He is her *father*!" Lydia whispered furiously, making the word itself an answer to my complaint. "And he knows she is safe here and well cared for and that she is learning godly ways."

"Tss!" It was all I could do to keep my voice low enough that Sister Olive would not hear. She had a great talent for listening to many things at the same time, especially things that might bring us later rebuke. "Lydia," I said, "you heard Mr. and Mrs. Gatwood speak their warning. And it was you yourself told me about the poisoned horse. How can you be sure that any of us is safe here? Ever since Mary's mother spoke of the danger, I have—" That was when I truly heard myself, when I knew that silence would have served me better.

"You spoke to that wicked woman?" Lydia regarded me as if I had just admitted to a great sin.

For time, for a moment to think, I cast my gaze down into my lap. We were in the loft, our assigned place, and in the momentary silence both of us kept, I heard the spatter of rain above me on the roof and the soft drone of voices in the house below. Months of my own silent misery were wrapped into the blanket where I sat; Mary had lain hidden beneath it only a few nights before, leaving some trace of her own distress. It was not a place that could hold much more unhappiness, I thought.

I glanced up at Lydia, whose mouth was still agape, and then back down at my apron. "Yes," I said, "I did see Mary's mother and I did talk to her, and I told no one. This is the wrong I confess." I did not think, of course, that I had done any wrong in speaking to Mrs. Bay, so it was my confession itself that would want confessing because it was a lie of sorts. My mother would not have approved, but Lydia did. When I looked up at her again, her face was quivering with interest.

"Where?" she demanded. "When?"

I took a breath. "I am afraid to confess such details to you," I said. "It might in some way make you an accomplice and bring harm to your soul. I want your soul to be at ease, Lydia. You should have your turn now and practice your confession to me." Then a truly wicked impulse came to me. "But then," I said, "you are always so careful, so good." I looked straight into her eyes. "Likely you have kept your mind on godly things all the time, even when those Gatwood fellows stared at you."

The light was not too dim to see the flush that started from her neckpiece and blazed up across her cheeks and forehead to the very roots of her hair. She stifled a little cry with one hand and covered her eyes with the other. It was a far better distraction than I had hoped.

"I confess," Lydia whispered. "I confess to

impure thoughts. I am bedeviled by dreams of Joseph Gatwood. He causes unease in my mind and unwelcome feelings in my physical person."

"Joseph Gatwood?" It was my turn to gape, not because I thought attraction was a sin but because I thought Joseph Gatwood a most unlikely target. I nearly pitied her, poor goose that she was, but I had to bite the inside of my lip to force away a smile. And then I began to see how her mortification could be at that moment my good fortune.

"Lydia," I said after she had sniffled for a moment, "I cannot think that we are ready, either of us, to tell these transgressions to Sister Olive. We should first make our own prayers and find the right words, don't you think?"

"I could never, ever tell," Lydia said, wiping her wet cheeks with the back of her hand.

"Well, then," I said, "these words have been between us only."

She wrinkled her forehead. "But, Susannah, it is different for you—"

I shook my head. "No, Lydia. If your confession is to be secret for a time, then so is mine. I will not speak of your sin"—I spoke the word firmly—"and you will not speak of mine."

She twisted her fingers together and apart and together again. "All right," she said at last. "But then we have nothing to say to Sister when she calls us."

I smiled. "Of course we do. Twice this week I picked blossoms at the edge of the woods when I had other chores to do. And I let the little girls finish their prayers early almost every day. You will think of something," I said.

Lydia had recovered herself enough to give her head a little toss. "I suppose," she said.

Relief was the strongest feeling in me that day, for I thought that no one should know of my meeting with Mary's mother. Sister Olive would keep me always in her sight if she found out, I was sure, and then I would be no better off than a bird in a cage. Yet it galled me that I had given away this weapon against me. And to Lydia.

S I X

The last days of spring that year were warm and bright. When they passed without any harm coming to us, I was lulled away from my worry by the small pleasures of the season. I led Sister Olive to believe that I had grown careless with the cooking, knowing that my punishment would be long hours in the garden. Truth to tell, I loved the sun on my back and the smell of green on my fingers. In the garden I would think of my mother, how she tended our plants at home, humming as she worked, pausing over beetles and tiny colored stones. "What an amazing wee thing!" she would say. "What a handiwork of God!" In Sister Olive's garden I was almost content, feeling that my mother was near and the Great Creator also.

The sanctity of such moments was easily broken, most often by Lydia, who contrived to be with me far more often than I would have liked. "Have you seen that woman today?" she would hiss at me from some rows over, and of course I had not, for of late Lydia had made sure that I had no opportunity. I had observed also that she and Abby both watched me sometimes when they had no call to do so, and thus I knew that Lydia must be poor at keeping secrets.

That was how the season passed until the Sunday I spoke to my father.

I had imagined this encounter for so long a time that I expected it to be in life just as it was in my mind. I knew the questions I would put to my father and the tone I must take in asking to be sent away from the Shakers. Perhaps he would come with me, I thought. I would plead for him to do so though I had little hope of it. Then, when the moment of our meeting came, I was so startled by the shape it took, so ill prepared, that I could scarcely speak at all.

It was a fair day, I remember, sometime in the month of June. I was distracted as we came to Meeting by the uncommon number of visitors milling about in the street. Even Sister Olive remarked aloud on it, she who had come to pride herself on keeping silence—her own and ours—all the way to Meeting. At first I was apprehensive, wondering if trouble might come in such a crowd. Then I had the thought that Mary's mother could be somewhere among the women, hiding her hair and her face under stylish headgear like any other visitor. After that I watched for her, turning my eyes this way and that as I took my place with the others moving along the path toward the women's door of the Meeting House.

What if Mrs. Bay looked for me, I thought, and saw me and did not know me? We had proper Shaker garments by then, all of us. I was dressed like Abby, and Abby was dressed like Jane, and Jane like Lydia, and Lydia like all the Sisters, old and young. Mary's mam could look straight at me and find not one thing to set me apart. At least that was what I feared. The thought so agitated me that I did not think to look for my father as I usually did when we filed into Meeting.

Except for the presence of so many spectators crowding the benches along the wall, there was no sign to me that this Sabbath Day would be different from the rest. We hung our bonnets on the appointed pegs, as usual, and sat in ranks, girls with the women, boys with the men. The floor seemed hard as ever as we sat for the songs and the speaking. Then the men took off their coats, and a group of Believers stood by the window, singing out a measured rhythm, and we all rose for the dance. I held my hands in front of me, palms up, like all the other dancers, and I moved through the familiar steps without thinking. I concentrated just enough in that press of women's bodies to avoid the flailing arms of a Sister who was suddenly possessed by the Spirit. Not long after, Lydia swooned, and one of the older Sisters tripped over her, but there was nothing new in that.

It was not until we were leaving, not until we were out in the street under the high sun that I saw my father. Sister Olive was fussing over Lydia, who was still quite pale and who staggered a bit as she walked. Neither of them noticed that I hung back as they moved on. I took a breath and shaped my mouth to say the word, to say "Father" as he moved toward me, but the sound stopped on my lips. His expression was forbidding. I thought he meant to shout at me.

"Susannah!"

But the voice came from behind me, and it was a woman's voice, quite old, with echoes that were strange to me.

"Is that really you, my child? William, is this the one?"

My father hurried, almost ran, to put himself between me and the figure that I turned to see.

"Oh, yes!" the woman cried. She leaned heavily on a walking stick, and her old face—the oldest I had ever seen—folded into countless tiny wrinkles as she beamed. "I would have known her any-where," she said to my father in her peculiar voice. "She has the curve of her mother's cheek. And the same eyes. Exactly."

I felt such a pang of pleasure and surprise in the midst of my general befuddlement that I could do no more than stare, mouth agape.

"Leave us," my father said to this wizened little woman. "Go. It is not fitting for visitors to detain Believers after worship."

"Posh!" She glanced toward other groups of two and three and four with heads bent for talk. Shakers were meant to file back to their dwellings in silence after Meeting, or such was the official rule. In truth many conversations with the world took place then. I closed my mouth firmly so as not to smile.

"William Arden," she said, "you were always such a straight stick of a man. I could never under-stand what dear Mariah saw in you."

My father's face turned the color of brick, and perhaps mine did also. All these months I had not heard my mother's name, had not even spoken it in silence to myself.

"I believe you have outlived your good man-ners," my father said to her.

"Quite so." She nodded. "At this point in my life I have more need of truth than of soothing words. And the truth is, William, that you should greet me with the respect due my age and family connection. Besides which, I have endured a journey that brought me great personal discomfort, and for the sole purpose of speaking with you face-to-face."

My father turned to me, and now he was pale. "Your place is with Sister Olive," he said. "Go there at once."

"But—I—she—" My tongue reached for words and could not find two that fit together. "Please," I whispered.

"This concerns her, William, as you must know." The woman turned her kindly eyes full on my face. "I have come to take her home with me, as her mother would have wanted."

A little cry escaped my lips. I could not help it. Heads turned in our direction.

"No!" he said. "There is no chance of that. I brought her here to protect her from the pain of the world, and surely that is what her mother would have wanted."

The old face grew softer as she studied his. "Poor William," she said. "But you are so mistaken. Everyone has pain. It proves we're alive. And in trying to hide this child away, you have brought her into danger."

My breath quickened. "There are rumors—" I began, but my father silenced me with a look.

"God protects his own," my father said, "and so

we are safe. Believers have no fear of rumors nor any time for careless tongues."

"Consider this," she said, fumbling with her sleeve and producing a folded paper. "I have brought you a copy of the *Western Star*, which is published in the town just up the way."

That was Lebanon, I knew, where most of the Gatwoods lived. And Mary's mam. I held my breath.

"Now, William," she said, her finger tapping the page, "a Colonel Smith writes here a list of dreadful things about this place. Perhaps they are true; perhaps they are not. What matters is that people may believe them and be angry. There will be much indignation against your Shakers, William. I have engaged a lawyer and made inquiries about Colonel Smith. This may be none too safe a place as the season goes along."

I thought I saw a shadow cross my father's face, but he expressed no dismay. "Foolish talk," he said curtly. He took the paper from her and put it inside his coat without so much as a glance at the words.

"I think she speaks truly," I whispered, trying not to tremble. "I—I have heard that we might have reason to be afraid."

"Susannah!" My father's voice held reproof. "Are you not a better Believer than that?"

"A Believer is a hard thing to be," I said, "when I

don't know what may happen next, and when I am so lonely." I could feel my chin coming up of its own accord. "I did not choose to be a Shaker."

The woman struck her walking stick against the ground. "For the love of God, William, do as I have begged in every letter. Let her be released to me!"

I could only stare, but my father almost smiled at her. "It is for the love of God that I will keep her here! You may have the lawyer, Margaret, but the law favors me. I am her father."

Margaret! The name clattered in my head like a clapper in a bell.

She made a sound of disgust and fixed my father with a baleful look. "Be steadfast, child," she said to me, although her eyes were still on him. "I do not give up easily." Then she moved away, slowly, using her stick, to join a man who waited for her by the Meeting House fence.

I watched her out of sight. "Who?" I breathed. "Who is she?"

My father considered for so long that I feared he would not answer at all. Then he sighed. "She is your mother's aunt Margaret," he said. "From Philadelphia."

I was shamed by the way the tears came down along my nose. "Why did Mother never speak of her?"

He frowned and said nothing.

I wiped one hand across my face, like a little child, and began again. "You said once that you should have sent me to her."

"No," he said quickly. "You must have dreamed that." And he turned on his heel and left me there.

SEVEN

*A*ll the way back to Sister Olive's that day, the day that I spoke to my father, hope and despair fluttered together like two birds in the tight cage of my chest. Yes, there was a place for me, but no, I could not go to it. My mother's aunt had come for me, had come far to find me. Frail as she was, she seemed full of the same spirit that had marked my mother. Yet my father appeared unassailable in his opposition to her. I could not think why he would feel so or why he should have so little care for my own wishes. I grew angry thinking of it, though I knew anger to be a sin that opened the door to wicked deeds. Even so, my mind raced on. Why could I not just flee this place? Why not go to my great-aunt Margaret, if I could discover where she was lodging, and then on to her home in Philadelphia? I shuddered, remembering the trip from Kentucky: the deep-night darkness of the forest, the far-off howling, and my father's gun so close beside him.

Then I saw the little house beyond the garden plot, and I took great pains to calm myself. I thought I could not bear to reveal these new things that troubled me to anyone, least of all to Lydia. But it was later than I thought; the door stood open to catch the breeze, what little there was, and I could see the table laid and everyone seated around it for the midday meal. I stepped across the threshold just as Sister Olive intoned the last word of thanks for the Sabbath food. Everyone looked up at once, and there I was, tardy.

Olive glared at me. Lydia and Abby exchanged knowing glances. The little girls, with their backs to me, turned their heads to see what was happening. Mary scooted over to make room on the end of the bench beside her. "I knew you would come," she said to me in a whisper that everyone could hear. I tried to smile at her, but I made a poor job of it.

Sister Olive could not punish me with garden work because it was the Sabbath. She did set me the task of straightening after the meal, directing me to do alone the work that three of us usually shared. Afterward she said I must think on my transgressions, numerous as they might be, in solitude, a circumstance that was more blessing than punishment to me even though the heat of the loft made my stomach churn. I had barely begun to sort my thoughts there under the low roof when Olive herself came to the foot of the ladder and called me down.

"I fear you will lie to me," she said, "so I choose not to ask if you loitered after Meeting to hatch some plot with the Bay woman."

My astonishment must have been written in my face, for Sister Olive nodded her head. "I see you did not expect to be found out," she said in her gloomiest, no-salvation voice. "Much as I pray for your soul, child, I do not know which way to turn to help you save it."

I could see that I was expected to reply to this, and meekly, but I could not hold back my agitation. "I beg you, Mrs. Gatwood, leave my soul alone," I said. "It would be the saving of me if I could go away from here!"

Sister Olive made a sound in her throat. "I knew you were rebellious," she said. Horror and satisfaction mingled in her voice. "I knew you were willful. But I never before thought you to be ungodly. I will not suffer this alone!"

For a moment, when she jerked my elbow and pulled me out of the house, I wondered if the stories told by the world's people could be true. It was whispered among the children that visitors said the Believers whipped and beat their young charges. Although I had seen no such thing, the very thought of it made me ill at ease all the while we trudged the mile and more from the Gatwood house to the Elders' Family dwelling. There Sister Olive demanded that Eldress Ruth be summoned away from her own meditations. I stood straight and still in the entry hall, just inside the women's door, a place that felt to me nearly as public as the Meeting House. Mrs. Gatwood leaned close to the Eldress as she recited a loud list of complaints against me, some warranted, some imagined.

"She dawdles," Sister Olive said, "and she dissembles. And, I grieve to say, this one does not confess her heart. She thinks to have secrets before God and the Believers, though she may have been led to it by that evil Sarah Bay. A bad apple like this may rot my whole barrel, may it not?"

I watched the eyes of Eldress Ruth widen ever so slightly. Then she nodded, seriously, and inclined her head to Sister Olive. "Thank you, Sister, for bringing this difficulty to my attention," she said. I had a moment of wild hope when I thought perhaps I would be found so wanting that I would be dismissed, *sent away*.

Sister Olive threw up her hands, palms heavenward. "What shall I do?" she cried.

Eldress Ruth smiled. "Why not go back to your

other charges now? You do very important work, Sister, and I'm sure someone is needing you. Leave this one with me for just a while. I had meant to send for her, anyway."

I stiffened, but it was only when the Eldress turned her smile to me that I realized I had been holding my breath. She opened the door to a small side room and pointed to a chair. There were only benches for the girls at Sister Olive's; I had not felt a real chair at my backside since Kentucky, since I had watched by my mother's bed.

"Come in, child," Eldress Ruth said. "Sit down. I understand there was a visitor at Meeting who wanted to speak to you."

"Yes, ma'am." I sat, scarcely surprised that she knew, for my words with my family earlier that day had been far from private.

There was a little silence, during which the Eldress's face grew sober. "Tell me," she said.

I took a breath. "I wanted to greet my father," I said carefully, "but a visitor, a woman, approached us just then, and—" I saw that the watching eyes were kind, and then I, who had learned to say so little about what was important to me, blurted out the truth that was in my heart. "And she is my mother's aunt Margaret from Philadelphia, and she wants me to come live with her. And I want that, too. She is my family."

Eldress Ruth shook her head. "We are your family," she said. "All of us. We are Believers together in the family of God, secure in the protection of our Heavenly Father and of Mother Ann." She reached across the short space between our two chairs and took one of my hands in both of her own. Her fingers were rough, for not even an Eldress could escape her share of chores, but the touch was warm.

"Begging your pardon, ma'am, it is the other kind of family that I crave. My aunt Margaret said that my mother would have wanted me to go to her. And I know that must be true."

"Dear Susannah," the Eldress said, "none of us can know what your mother would have wanted. We all must learn to put away our grief for those who make the happy journey before us. And then we must go on to live as pure a life, as holy a life, as we can." There was such feeling in her voice, such welcome comfort in her tone, that I nearly missed her meaning.

"Would my life be impure if I lived it with Aunt Margaret?" I asked. Though I supposed it to be an impudent question, my only rebuke was in the withdrawal of Eldress Ruth's warm hands, which she folded in her lap.

"The world is fraught with temptations, child, and overrun with evils that you cannot yet name."

I shook my head, mute. The world I remembered

had laughter in it, and stories, and love. My mother had loved me, and I her. Silent though I was, Eldress Ruth seemed to know my mind.

"Some Believers feel it is a great burden to give up their ties to the family of the flesh," she said, "but those ties are distractions, child, as you will come to see. If you give your heart to another—a kinswoman now, perhaps a husband one day—how can you then give your heart to God?"

I thought to myself that God might not reject the gift of a heart that also loved others. My mother had long before taught me that the store of kindness in the world can never be depleted, for it is giving it away that makes it grow. I did not say any of this to Eldress Ruth. To her I said, "The choice is very hard."

She smiled then. "There is no choice for you now, Susannah. You are fortunate to have an earthly father who has chosen well on your behalf. He has told Elder David not more than an hour ago that he intends for you to stay among the Believers."

I put my hands to my face, for I did not want her to see what I felt.

"It is his choice, my child, by moral law and by the laws of the state. You must accept what you cannot change." The Eldress sighed. "And I am afraid it is also your duty to accept this gift with gratitude and a cheerful heart."

I stood up, unbidden. "And must I be cheerful, too, when Colonel Smith comes for his grandchildren and I must stay behind? Or when something violent happens because people in the countryside have such dreadful suspicions about this place? I have heard—"

"Quiet yourself, Susannah!" Her voice was low but the tone severe. "You have heard too much. I am sorry if you have been taken in by rumors. So much idle talk, such wicked mischief! You are not to speak of it. The little children should never hear a breath of it."

I did not tell her that they had been frightened for weeks, though of what they were not sure.

"Go back to Sister Olive," she said more calmly. "Be useful. I think you are her best help. Even so, when you have learned to curb your tongue a bit, I will bring you to live in the Children's Family. Your faith will strengthen there."

The very thought of the Children's Family filled me with dismay. I imagined it as Lydia many times over, plus boys of all sizes, causing their own kind of commotion in the other side of the house. After that I could not bring one single mannerly word of leave-taking to my lips; instead, I nodded to the Eldress and bolted from the room.

But I did not weep as I fled along the path. I planned.

EIGHT

*S*o slow were my steps and so deep my thoughts that day that the sun dropped behind the trees before I reached the Gatwood house. It was too late for Sunday supper, too early for evening prayers, the best time of the week. By Sister Olive's own decree, this was the hour that children in her care could put away their chores and the rigors of the faith to amuse themselves, but quietly. On fine evenings like this one all the girls would be outside, the house empty save for Sister Olive. Good, I thought. Lydia would not have to hear the painful words I had chosen to say.

I found Mrs. Gatwood near the door where she had pulled her chair into the light to read the pamphlet she held at arm's length. Eyes squinting behind her spectacles, she smiled and nodded as she read. It was a wonder to me that the beliefs that gave her so much pleasure in meditation made her so intractable and ill humored in their practice.

"Sister," I whispered, and she looked up, smile fading. I took a deep breath. "I am sorry if I have brought you grief," I said. In some part that was true, for my mother had taught me to bring deliberate offense to no one. But now it was also part of my design to appear to be more content among the Shakers.

Mrs. Gatwood took a moment to study my expression. "The Eldress has set you on the narrow path, I see," she said with evident satisfaction. "Good. Now go on. It will soon be time to fetch in the little ones."

Even though my murmured answer was obedient, I thought I felt her eyes still on me as I hurried around the corner of the house. Did she surmise somehow that my haste was all to locate Mary, to whisper alone to her, to discover if she could help me find her mother again? Although the plan I had formed was only the first tender shoot of an idea, Mary's mam was important to it.

"Susannah!" Lydia called to me from the stump where she and Abby sat with their heads together. "Where were you today?"

Somehow it was harder to be civil with Lydia

than to be contrite before Sister Olive. "Eldress Ruth wanted to see me," I said in as even a voice as I could manage.

Abby made a face, and Lydia sniffed in disbelief. For my part I pretended not to notice. "Where is Mary?" I said.

"With the others." Abby fluttered her hand toward the woodlot.

"Don't worry about them," Lydia called after me. "Jane went along."

I was reassured by that, for Jane was a cheerful little soul and handy with the younger ones. When I found her at the edge of the woodlot plaiting neck-laces of grass, there were three small girls waiting to try them on and then fling them away. Jane was old enough to know that proper Believers wore no orna-mentation. Celia squealed when she saw me and came running, and the others followed—Elizabeth, Betsy, and then Jane. The little ones hugged my skirts, and I bent down to embrace them all, for on that dreadful day I was grateful for any offer of affection.

"Where's Mary?" I said when I had finished admiring their necks.

"She went back," two said at once.

"Maybe to Abby." Jane pointed the way I had come. "She said she wanted someone to play the guessing game with her."

I frowned; it was I who had taught the little ones the best questions for I Spy. Sometimes we played in whispers to make their chores go faster while Sister Olive's back was turned. "But I have just seen Abby with Lydia," I said, "and there was no sign of Mary."

"She'll be in the house then," Jane suggested. "Won't she?"

"Or in the privy," said Celia, smiling wide enough to crinkle her round cheeks.

I nodded, but my heart was thumping. "I'll go back then," I said, "and find her. Mind you remember to come in before the sun is all the way behind the trees."

I felt in my heart that Mary was not with Sister Olive, but I hurried back to the house to make certain. I worried how I would explain my search, for I feared Olive would immediately think that Mary's mother had snatched her away and that I had been an accomplice.

"Sister," I began, and then covered the sound of the word with my hand, for Mrs. Gatwood's chin rested now on her bosom, and her eyes were closed. Gratefully I picked my way around her sleeping form and went to the loft, where I turned back every blanket and peered into the chimney corners in case Mary was playing a hiding game. Truth to tell, I wondered myself, as I searched, if Mrs. Bay might have come to the woodlot and somehow, unbeknownst to Jane and the others, signaled to her little daughter. Such an idea should make me happy, I realized. Was it not a dearest wish of mine that Mary should be with her mother? And yet, and yet, if Sarah Bay had no reason to return to the Shaker settlement, I would have no hope of enlisting her aid on my own behalf, and that was the largest part of my plan.

I did not find Mary in the house that day, or in our little privy, or in the shed. I began to imagine then that Lydia and Abby had hidden her away to tease me, and I went back to the stump to confront them. Their faces told me otherwise.

"Ha!" Lydia said. "You know her mother must have taken her. That wicked woman! You *must* know, Susannah!" She looked with knowing eyes from me to Abby and back again, but I was too troubled to rise to her bait.

"What if her mother *didn't* take her?" I countered.

"Could she be lost?" Abby said.

I shook my head. I could scarcely bear to think of it. There was no way to know what dangers lurked in the world beyond the woodlot. Great cats, perhaps, or vipers. People who meant harm to the Shakers. Sharp rocks and fallen branches and who could say what else?

"Maybe I can find her," I said, but my heart was racing.

"I am going to the house to tell Sister Olive," Lydia said.

"No!" I said quickly. "Please. We must hurry and look for her while it is still light." Even Lydia could see the sense in that, and so the three of us set to work.

We searched and called through the woodlot, collecting all manner of snags in our clothing that had to be mended later. I remember the heat of that evening and the mosquitoes that buzzed at my damp forehead and at the bare skin on the back of my neck. I remember how my stomach pinched, reminding me that I had missed my supper, and how every shadowed bush and stump became Mary in my mind. I remember shouting her name until my tongue was too dry to form another word. But we did not find her.

The dark came down and caught us, and then Sister Olive had to be told, and Brothers had to be summoned from the Elders' Family. I was not allowed to take the message, for by then I was weeping and could not stop. The men came with lanterns and torches, fanning out in every direction from the Gatwood house. All of us girls were banished to the loft while they were about.

"Pray," directed Sister Olive. "Beseech our Lord to keep his little lamb from harm. Pray hard. Lydia will lead you."

That stopped my tears and my own silent prayers, the ones that had been tumbling through my head since we began to search. My supplications would likely go unheard now, I thought, with Lydia making so much noise in the ear of God. Besides, I was spent. I turned my attention to comforting Celia, who whimpered in heat and distress. I crouched beside her to stroke her head and discovered a crack far down in the wall that afforded a good view of the dooryard, where two of the Brothers waited with a lantern. One of them stood with his head bowed; I recognized him from Meetings as Brother Richard, who often did the speaking. The other man paced beside him, stopping now and again to say a word or two. When Lydia's prayer ended with a yawn, and the loft grew quiet except for sniffs and fidgets, I began to listen for their voices. I heard Brother Richard come to our door finally and tell Sister Olive she should sleep, that someone would awaken her if the child were found. A short time after that the Brothers began to straggle back, shaking their heads and looking for the water jug.

"Nothing," they said to one another. "There is nothing to be found."

"Naught but an owl."

"Brother Amos caught his toe in a root and twisted his leg."

"A man cannot see beyond his nose in that thicket, I tell you."

I saw Brother Richard raise his hand for silence and turn to his companion. "Brother Thomas," he said, "as the child's father, do you give your leave for us to halt this search until first light?"

My breath caught in my throat. I had not recognized Thomas Bay in the faint glow of the lantern.

"My thanks to you, Brothers," he said, "but I fear this effort was doomed at the start. It is all too possible that her mother has taken her and that you have sacrificed your rest for nothing."

After that came a general rumbling of voices, and the dim lights began to move away from the house. Someone knocked below, and I heard Sister Olive murmuring, and then all was silence.

So, I thought, perhaps Mary really was with her mother. I realized all at once the depth of my own weariness—the weakness of my limbs, the stiffness of my neck, the ache in my breast. I would shut my eyes, I thought, and go to sleep and let my life unfold as it would, for I was a child and I had no plan. There was nothing else I could do. I struggled to make a better spot for myself on the floor beside Celia, and I touched her cheek good-night, thinking of Mary.

An idea came to me then so unbidden, so swift and sure that I knew I must not sleep. I must act.

There was no need to dress, for I had not bothered to remove so much as one petticoat. I felt my way out of the loft, crawling around and between the other girls to place my feet carefully on the ladder, step after step. I strained to see the thicker blackness that would be Sister Olive's bedstead, for I had no wish to fall into her on my way to the door. In a moment I had let myself out into the night, where the rush of fresh, cooler air brought me full awake. I picked my way as fast as I could, telling myself not to be frightened. Insects were chirring, and a nightbird called, far away. I did see two pairs of glowing eyes, but they were tiny eyes, low to the ground. I had liked the dark in Kentucky, I reminded myself, had coaxed my mother to sit with me and watch for falling stars. The dark was better with two, I thought. All the more reason to hurry.

I stumbled along the path toward the village, falling more than once, but without harm. At last, when I was nearly convinced that I had taken a wrong turn, I found what I was seeking. Without light, it was my nose rather than my eyes that gave first warning. The Elders' huge barn loomed up ahead of me, solid darkness against the star-pricked sky behind it. I was careful then, hoping not to startle any of the creatures. I held up my skirts and made for the small door I had often noted at the side, calling, "Mary, Mary," in a soft singsong.

The smells of new hay and manure were strong in the air that greeted me. A horse whickered. I knew enough to stand for a moment to get the feel of this new blackness, and then I crept soft and easy along the rows of stalls, whispering Mary's name.

"Mary? Are you here? Mary!" Far at the other end of the barn a cow bawled quietly, as if in answer. I began to feel foolish. Two steps more, and I cracked my shin against a pail. I stifled my yowl of pain, but there was still a commotion—some stamping of hooves, snuffling, snorting. And then a whimper.

"Mary?"

Another whimper.

I held myself perfectly still. "Mary? Where are you?"

"Here." The voice was behind me. I turned and backtracked in the dark, crooning her name all the while so she would know I was coming close.

"Here," she said again, and then I found her, curled up on a piece of rough blanket at the end of a stall. I went down on my knees and pulled her to me.

"Mary!" I whispered. "Everyone has been looking for you! I was so worried, I—"

She drew a long, shaky breath; I could feel her little chest rise and fall against mine. "Where did you go, Susannah?" she said. "Why didn't you come back?"

"Oh, Mary," I said, "I did come back. I—I was just . . . slow."

She sniffled and put her face against mine. "I came to look for you at that place we went before. But there were too many people and then I came to look at the horses and someone shut the door and it was dark and—"

"Shush," I said. "It's all right, little one. Don't cry."

I do not know to this day how I found my way back through the dark of that barn, how I managed that trip to Mrs. Gatwood's house with Mary in my arms and nothing but starlight to show me the path. I do remember that Sister Olive was sitting by the door when we came and that one of our precious candles burned in her hand. By its light I saw a glint of tears on one of her puffy cheeks. I know she spoke to me, for her mouth moved; but I do not know what tone was in her voice that night. I was too tired to listen. I stumbled past Sister Olive and lowered Mary onto her cot. Then I sank down onto the floor beside her and was asleep in an instant.

*A*fter that night Mary became my shadow, ever as close to my hand as a pocket. For the most part it was by her own choice, although it was also Sister Olive's directive.

"Keep that child *always* in your sight," Olive said to me that next day after Mary was lost. She made it sound as if I should have more blame for Mary's absence than credit for her discovery. I did not bother to protest, for I was barely awake when she said it. Even so, the sun had long been up. I had already been required to give my halting account of the night's events. Lydia had already told us, twice, about meeting the Brethren on the path at dawn and how they praised God to hear that little Mary had not been stolen away after all. According to Lydia, there was no need for me to make too much of my starlight search; the men would have found Mary, anyway, she said, when they did their morning chores.

Although I could not deny this, I might still have said something to cause me regret had not one of the younger Sisters from the Elders' Family come just then. She brought our basket of eggs, a small bag of meal, and a message that Sister Olive was to go speak to the Eldress.

I saw Olive's forehead draw into puckers. "I do all I can," I heard her whisper to Lydia when the young Sister had gone. "The Eldress knows a woman my age was not meant to see after all these children."

By that I knew Sister Olive did feel some small measure of guilt in Mary's disappearance, but it was little comfort to me as I took up my chores. The weariness of the night just past and of the day before still hung on me, slowing my steps and clouding my thoughts. Abby complained so of my clumsiness with the breakfast kettle that I left it for her to clean. As soon as Sister Olive straightened her apron and marched off to see the Eldress, I took Mary by the hand and escaped into the garden.

Gratefully I sank down among bean leaves and began to search out the weeds that struggled helter-skelter for space among our tidy plants. My mind worked as slowly as my hands that morning, and so my thoughts did not fall into good order until I was halfway through the beans, between green corn and squash. Where had my aunt Margaret passed the night? I wondered.

"Mary," I said, remembering all at once that I had questions for her. Then I paused, for I did not know how to ask them. She was standing close by, cradling something put together of twigs and leaves, and when I spoke her name, she took a step toward me.

"See my baby?" she said.

I swallowed, for something in the sight of her with so poor a toy made a catch in my throat.

"Mary," I said, fumbling for words, "do you remember a long time ago when we saw your mam?"

She turned her wide eyes toward mine too quickly and too bright with hope. But I pressed on.

"Does she still come here sometimes? To the woodlot?" I dropped my voice to a whisper, though no one was likely to hear us. "I would like to see her."

Mary shook her head slowly and let go of the twig-baby so that it fell at her feet. "I would like to see her, too," she said, looking so suddenly wretched that I motioned her down into my lap.

We sat that way a long time, keeping silent about our own sorrows, doing nothing. I traced the curve of Mary's cheek with one of my weed-stained fingers, thinking how just yesterday my aunt Margaret had seen my mother's face in my own. If only I could find Margaret, I thought, I would tell her how much I wanted to be with someone who knew my mother's face. With family. I would leave Turtle Creek with Margaret, I vowed, no matter what my father said, no matter what the Eldress said. If only I could see her again to tell her this. If only I could send her this message. If only Mary's mam would come to the woodlot. The more I thought on it, the more I was certain that only Sarah Bay could help me.

Yet it was not Sarah Bay who appeared at the edge of the garden as I thought of her; it was the Gatwoods, three of them. Mr. and Mrs. Benjamin Gatwood were on foot, trudging through the morning's heat toward Sister Olive's door, with their grandson Joseph slouching behind. For a moment I could not fathom why there should be visitors at such a day and hour, but then I remembered that the Gatwoods were town people. Perhaps their chores arranged themselves around a different clock, I thought. For another thing, the old couple seemed agitated. They spoke low to each other and shook their heads and gestured as if surrounded by things unseen.

None of the Gatwoods could see Mary and me, for the bean plants grew tall and lush with leaves along the poles that supported them. I put my finger to my lips as a signal to Mary, and thus hidden, we crept as close to the house as we dared. Mr. Gatwood paused near the apple tree and called out to to his sister-in-law.

"Olive!" he shouted. "Olive Gatwood! Come out so we may talk to you!"

It was Lydia who came to the doorway. "God's greeting, sir," she said, prim as you please, "but Sister Olive is away for a bit." She nodded to Mrs. Gatwood and took a breath that puffed her up even more than usual. "I am in charge," she announced, and then I saw her look over Mrs. Gatwood's head and catch sight of Joseph. Lydia's cheeks went scarlet, and she made a little choking sound.

"Are you all right, dear?" Mrs. Gatwood asked, taking a few steps forward. "You must be burning up in there," she said. "Just look at your face! Come out here in the air."

"N-no," stammered Lydia. "No, I cannot. I—I am required to stay in the house." I noted that small untruth with satisfaction, thinking ahead to the next week's confessions.

"When is Olive coming back then?" Mr. Gatwood wanted to know, apparently unmoved by Lydia's distress. "We have brought something she must see."

Abby's head popped up over Lydia's shoulder.

"Can you wait?" she said. "It will only be a short time."

Lydia's body sagged against the doorframe. "Oh, no," she said, "you must not wait." Joseph had stopped well behind the elder Gatwoods, and I could see clearly how he winked at Lydia. "Can you not just leave this thing for Sister Olive to see?" she said.

"It is no small matter!" said Mr. Gatwood with great emphasis. "And there should be no delay. We came at our first opportunity." He pulled something from beneath his coat, and I caught my breath to see a paper just like the one my aunt Margaret had given to my father. "I need to look her in the eye while we speak of this," Mr. Gatwood said. "It is my duty to make her finally listen to reason!" He was not quite shouting, although his wife was motioning for him to be quiet.

"That is something between you and Sister Olive," Lydia said, keeping her eyes cast down. Much as it might give the appearance of humility, I knew her guarded glance was meant to protect her from Joseph's brazen stare.

Eunice Gatwood put her hand on her husband's arm. "It *is* important," she said to the girls in the doorway. "It is a matter of safety that concerns you all."

Lydia shook her head. "Come back when Sister

Olive is here," she said. I had to bite my tongue there among the bean rows to keep from calling out. Regardless of Joseph Gatwood, it seemed to me that Lydia was empty-headed, with no more curiosity than a cat. Surely Sister Olive should know what was in the *Western Star*, and if those words were to incite more hatred against Turtle Creek, I thought everyone should know about them.

"Come back another time," Lydia insisted.

The Gatwoods did not leave but stood whispering together in the dooryard. Lydia and Abby withdrew into the dim house, but they took turns peeking out, and each time I saw Lydia it seemed more likely she would fall in a faint. Behind his grandparents, Joseph Gatwood turned two cartwheels and stood on his head. I had to hold Mary's face against my skirts to keep her from giggling. Finally it was Jane who came to the door of the house.

"Lydia says, please go away now," she said, calm as always. "We are not supposed to have the world's people in our dooryard bothering us."

Joseph, right side up, waggled his ears. Even I stared in fascination.

"*Bothering* you!" sputtered Mr. Gatwood. But he failed to go on with whatever else he was ready to say when he saw how young Jane was.

"We'll go!" Mrs. Gatwood called, and then, in a

gentler tone, she said, "Poor Olive! What a life she has made for herself." She looked around at Joseph then, catching him in a moment of good behavior. "Come along, Joseph," she said. "Deliver your grandfather's paper up to the young lady at the door."

By the time he had taken those few steps that were required, Jane had gone in and Lydia had started out. And so it was into Lydia's hand that Joseph Gatwood placed the *Western Star* and into Lydia's eyes that Joseph Gatwood looked at that moment.

I knew what would happen. It was my good fortune, though, that Lydia had a firm grip on the door. The Gatwoods had turned their backs on the house and were well away before I heard the soft thump that was Lydia falling and the muffled cries of alarm from the little girls. Then an idea came to me. The Gatwoods knew Mary's mother. Mrs. Gatwood might take her a message. I seized the moment.

"Run, Mary!" I said softly. "Dip the gourd into the rain barrel, and take the water to Abby! And then stay in the house. I'll be there in just a few minutes."

"No!" She clung to my arm. " I want to stay with you."

"Please, Mary, it's only for a little bit. The other girls need you. Lydia needs a wet cloth on her forehead—poor Lydia!—and you will be the one with the water." It took a moment to convince her and two more to watch her to the door, and by that time the Gatwoods had walked far enough to be out of my sight, beyond the elderberries at the end of the garden.

I ran to catch up. I could not shout for Mrs. Gatwood to wait, much as I longed to do so, because someone at the house would surely hear. I ran faster and took such a stitch in my side that I had to limp along then, clutching my middle and straining to hear their voices over the rasp of my own breath. Such was my condition when Joseph popped out from behind a tree and barred my way.

"Please," I said, "I need to talk to your grandmother."

"You go away now," he said, mocking Jane. "The world's people are not to have Believers following them and bothering them."

"Let be!" I said shortly, for I was weary of his fooling. "Jane is naught but a child, and anyway, I am not a Believer." I took a breath. "Not quite, anyway."

Joseph Gatwood's eyebrows rose almost high enough to meet his hair. "What do you want with my grandmother?" he said, still blocking the way by which I could go to her.

"I hoped she would speak to Mrs. Bay on my behalf," I said, surprised by my own candor. "I need to know if she can help me find my great-aunt Margaret, who traveled a very long way to see me at Meeting yesterday and maybe to take me home with her, but I do not know where she is now—" When I stopped to take a breath, I noticed that he looked at me with something new in his eyes, a glint that was akin to sympathy.

"What is the rest of her name, this Margaret?"

I bit my lip, and he could see I did not know. "She is from Philadelphia," I said instead. "A tiny old woman who walks with a stick. I think Mary's mam could help me find her. I hope she could. I wanted someone to ask Mrs. Bay would she please come to Meeting if she could and wait for me in the woodlot afterward. Please," I said. "Could you tell your grandmother all that? Would you?"

There was a burst of voices ahead of us then, and it was clear that Sister Olive had returned and would be coming any moment into our view, along with the elder Gatwoods. I knew I must fly to reach the house, to reach Mary, before I was found in such a transgression as this.

"Please tell her," I begged, too desperate to feel soiled by the begging.

In my last glimpse of Joseph Gatwood that day I saw a maddening grin spread across his face.

"I might," he said. "I just might."

T E N

For all that week and well into the next, Sister Olive grumbled even more than was her habit over her own tasks, and ours. She said not one word about her visit to the Eldress nor about her arguments with Benjamin and Eunice Gatwood on the day I had pleaded with Joseph about passing along my message. The Gatwoods had not come again, and as far as I could tell, their newspaper had completely disappeared. Over this I felt a great sense of loss, for I would have loved to read every word. I needed something to remind me that there was more in the world than Sister Olive's little house and the cluster of buildings near the Meeting House, and the path between.

My mother had kept a packet of faded newspapers, *Virginia Gazettes*, in the little leather trunk at the foot of her bed, where she stored the family treasures. I was given leave to read them from time to time and to ask for the stories of why she had saved them. My favorite came from the earliest issue and its item about a certain Governor's Ball. Virginia was still a colony then, my mother always said, and my grandmother was still a young woman, unmarried. Then she would begin a recitation, naming all the planters and merchants, all the wealthy and important men, who had danced with my grandmother that evening. What would it be like, I wondered, to dance to the sound of musicians playing rather than the drone of voices singing? What would it be like to wear a dress that shone by lamplight? Or to let my hand rest on the arm of a young man? I wondered if Aunt Margaret had also gone to the Governor's Ball and why my mother had never told me anything about her. Every day I remembered something of home; every day I tried to imagine the future.

At the end of that week I went to Meeting with a hopeful heart, thinking my aunt might again be in attendance, but she was not. My father was there, but he would not so much as meet my eyes. I contrived to be alone for a few moments on the path after the service, but Sarah Bay did not appear. I remember how fine the weather was, what fair days we had, so that we girls avoided the tortures of all-day mending and stitching that came with summer rain. Even so, the time seemed oppressive to me. Nothing happened, yet I hoped and feared for something to happen. Rescue and disaster seemed equal possibilities, and dreams haunted my sleep.

Then one morning, as we sat to breakfast, I sensed that something different was in the air. Sure enough, Sister Olive kept us in our places when the mush and milk were gone. She stared so hard at each of us in turn that everyone stopped fidgeting. Even Celia finished tugging at the edge of her cap and sat still for once.

"This is the day," Sister Olive told us, as if we knew already what she might mean. I felt a small stirring of apprehension, no more than a tingle.

"Eldress Ruth said Wednesday week," Olive said, "and that has come, and I have decided." Every line of her face bespoke determination.

I caught Abby's eye, and Jane's, and then Lydia's. I was not the only one who was puzzled.

"What is it that you have decided, Sister Olive?" Lydia asked after a moment when we all were silent. She used the oversweet tone with which she had addressed Sister Olive ever since her last encounter with Joseph Gatwood.

Olive rose abruptly. "Some of you are to go this

very day to live with the Children's Family."

No one spoke. I barely breathed.

"This afternoon you will wrap your Sabbath clothing in your bedcover and walk with me as far as the Elders' barn." She paused to scowl at Mary when she mentioned the barn. "One of the Sisters will meet you there and take you the rest of the way," Olive went on. "The others here will wash bedding and do it right smart to lay out and have dry by nightfall." She glared at us as if to question why we were not already at work.

"But who is to go?" said Jane at last.

"You, for one," Sister Olive said. "And Celia and Elizabeth. The three of you." She let her gaze move around the table. "This house was never meant to be a permanent home for you. Not for any of you. For all of you there will come a turn." Still, we all were silent, and I thought Olive's expression began to sag.

"Moving on to the Children's Family will be an important step for you," she said finally. "You are moving one bit closer to spiritual union with God and Mother Ann."

The little girls sat with their lips parted, uncomprehending.

My knees were weak with relief that she had not called my name, nor Mary's. If we were separated, I thought, I might never be able to convince Mary's mother to help me. Even so, I was not happy with Sister Olive's choosing. I would miss Jane and Celia, especially Celia, who often made me smile. I would be happier if I had to miss Lydia, I thought.

"Sister Olive," I said, "I think Lydia cares more than any of us for the things of the Spirit." I felt my cheeks flush, but I plunged right on. "Do you not think she also should deserve to take that step now?"

Sister Olive looked at me sharply. "I must keep Lydia here for a time," she said, "because this household needs at least one girl who knows what godliness is." Across the table Lydia glowed.

"And I must keep you," Olive said, fastening me with a look that felt like a pin, "because you are the burden that has been given me. Perhaps you will yet be a Believer in your heart, though I have my doubts." Under the edge of the table Mary reached for my hand.

"Do not think," Olive went on, stabbing the air with her finger word by word, "that I do not know how you have been tempted and how in your weakness you have flirted with those temptations."

I sighed. Eldress Ruth had surely told her about Aunt Margaret and my hopes of leaving.

"I will watch close over you," Sister Olive assured me, while the other faces at the table stared. "I will see that you are saved from this wicked world," she said. "You will not be idle here, and so you will not fall into sin."

I cast down my eyes because I could no longer bear to look at her, and somehow that satisfied her enough that she sent us all off, finally, to our tasks.

It was sad all that day, from breakfast to the leaving. Even now I carry a picture in my head of Celia at the end of a little procession in the late-day sun, trudging out of sight with her bundle dragging along behind. Mary stood on a stump and waved at them for a long time. Betsy stayed close, silent as usual, sucking two fingers. She and Elizabeth had been like shadows of each other, always together.

I thought to tell the little girls a story to ease their loneliness, but I had hardly begun when Lydia squawked at me from the window to come help with supper. I found Abby stirring up such a great crock of slapjack batter that I was aghast.

"Why do we need all this?" I protested. "There are not so many of us now, and you are making even more than usual."

Abby sniffed. "Sister Olive measured out the meal herself."

Lydia nodded. "And said to use an extra egg."

"There will be slapjacks forever," I said with disgust. Sister Olive's meals were filling but very tiresome. I wondered suddenly if the Sisters who saw to the cooking for the Children's Family had a lighter hand than Sister Olive. I allowed myself a moment to remember the biscuits that baked on my mother's hearth and the magic stewpot into which she could throw many bits of almost nothing and take out something fine. She never looked at a receipt, I knew. Her lists of ingredients and directions were stored in her head, and I grieved that I had not had time to learn them all. If I had, there might have been tastier fare at Sister Olive's table.

Such were my thoughts, these small complaints layered up to cover the hugeness of my discontent, when Mary came running into the house with Betsy panting just behind her.

"Sister Olive is back!" Mary fairly shouted, though we all were in touching distance. Her eyes seemed wild to me, their blue a bit lighter, the thin dark rim around the color that much darker. And her face was pale as moonlight.

"Whatever ails you?" Abby demanded of her.

"Sister Olive—" Mary began, but whatever else she might have said was muffled as she hid her face in my skirt.

"Little goose," Lydia said. "You knew Sister Olive was coming back. She—" Lydia turned toward the doorway and stopped in mid-sentence. Everything about her went still, and then finally she breathed and stepped back.

Sister Olive swept into her house. "Make sure

you set around all the spoons when you do the table," she said briskly. Behind her there were five new girls, little to big, in regular clothes. I knew in a moment their families had just come to the Shakers. I remembered how it was. Poor things, I said to myself. Poor things.

ELEVEN

*S*o began a long, unhappy time in the summer of that year, a waiting time when there was no news to be had of the Gatwoods or Mary's mam or my aunt Margaret, but a great deal of hard, hot work to do. It was only exhaustion that allowed me to sleep in the heat of that summer; I grew tired to the point of pain in the exertions Sister Olive set for me and the others, to keep us from sin. At Turtle Creek the air grew hot in the day and lay still upon us all night, heavy and flat as a blanket on a bed. I longed for the night breezes of the Kentucky hills.

And there was much sniffling in the darkness at that time as the new girls realized each night, again, that in spite of the crowd in Sister Olive's house, we were each of us alone. The smallest one, barely more than a baby, toddled cheerfully enough all day from one bit of mischief to another but wailed herself to sleep every night, not for lack of hands to comfort her but for want of a more familiar touch. The eldest of the new girls was Liza, Abby's twin in height, though not in demeanor. Liza was a slow and gentle spirit, full of gratitude for everything. I could tell by the way she praised Sister Olive's cooking that she had been eating at a poor table. At first I thought she might be a friend for me, but it was Lydia who claimed her ear whenever there was a chance for talk.

Of all the new girls, the three in-betweens took most of my attention, not because they were so sad by night, but because they were so insufferable by day. Darcy and Jennet were blood sisters, and I am ashamed to admit I envied them that. The other girl, Prudence, had lived in the same town, so Sister Olive said, and their two families had traveled together to Turtle Creek. All three girls were near in their ages to Betsy and to Mary and should have made them good companions, but those three clung together and could not make room in their little world for any but one another.

My mother had often told me that little children are so fresh from their Maker and so innocent that they must always be forgiven even as they are corrected. And so I was generous in my feelings toward Prudence and Jennet and Darcy all the while I helped Olive and Lydia scold them for whining and refusing their chores, for taunting and teasing, for throwing tiny green apples picked from Sister Olive's tree, even for putting a long-legged spider under Betsy's cap. I did not feel so generous when they began to make dangerous mischief.

One dull, hot day when all the little girls were assigned the task of chasing birds away from our garden, Mary came running into the house with wide eyes.

"Come see the smoke!" she urged. "Come outside!"

I had my hands in scrub water and my mind on other things, and so for that first moment I was not alarmed. "How can you watch over our vegetables if your eyes are on the chimney?" I said.

"No!" Her whole body bounced as she spoke. "Not from the chimney, Susannah!"

"Where then?" I knocked over the pail in my sudden haste to follow her. Sister Olive had left me in charge while she and the other older girls had gone to the Elders' Family, to help cook a meal for the hired hands working alongside the Brethren in the hayfield. I could not imagine how wildfire might have started, but it terrified me to think I might face it alone.

I bounded past Mary into the garden, where Betsy sat unmindful of the blackbirds with the baby sleeping on her lap.

"Over here!" Mary called. I turned my head and saw, finally, a thin wisp of smoke curling skyward from the other side of the house. My chest went tight. What if the house should burn? I tripped twice on my own feet rushing to the spot, and then I shrieked.

Prudence and Darcy and Jennet were hovered together over a fire of twigs just inches from the back wall of the house, pretending to bake hoecakes made of mud. When I rushed in to stamp out the little dancing flames and smother them with earth, the girls howled in protest. They would not have heard the things I needed to say to them even if I could have found the breath.

"Leave us alone!" said Darcy. "We never get to play."

Jennet's mouth was set into a sulk. "I want to go home."

Prudence studied my face. "Mary did it," she said. "You were busy, and she tiptoed into the house like this"—she paused to demonstrate—"and then she snitched some coals out of the fireplace and carried them out here on a little rock—see it?—so we could cook."

Beside me, Mary began to shake her head, but I

had no need of her denial. I could see whose fingers bore the telltale smudges of charred wood and whose were clean.

"Mary did it," Jennet repeated, and Darcy joined in, echoing the words while she rubbed her own palms against her skirt.

"Playing with fire is a wicked thing to do," I said passionately, and I think my face itself must have looked like flame. "Your skirts might have caught fire and burned your skin and brought you terrible pain." The three of them shared a sober look.

"But to play with fire and then *lie* about the fault!" I said. "Sister Olive will surely punish you."

And she did. In spite of the story that all of them tried to tell her about Mary, Sister Olive heard me out instead. Prudence and the sisters were told to stay inside the house for all that week, to keep busy with their chores, to speak no word of complaint, and to double their time for prayers. I was to be their overseer. It was more punishment for me than for them, I thought, and also for Mary, who was still my full-time charge and would not have ventured far from my sight in any case.

In the final reckoning it was poor Mary who suffered most, for from that time on she was the target for every little nuisance, every little harm that the three could imagine. They were like chickens in a henyard, pecking away at another without reason.

They would stop if scolded, but then the next attempt was more clever. Mary had a bee sting one day, which was no one's fault, but when I rolled her sleeve to put on a poultice, I found a cluster of ugly purple bruises.

"Darcy pinches," was all she would say, and so I asked Sister Olive if Mary could sleep in the loft with me. "To keep her out of trouble" was the way I phrased it, and Olive agreed. Lydia complained that with Liza we were already short of space, although her real meaning was that she did not want Mary to hear the way she sometimes whispered Joseph Gatwood's name as she fell to sleep. A little girl like Mary might mention such a thing at an awkward time. Lydia had practiced confessing it to me because it was good for her soul, she said, but she was not yet ready to tell Sister Olive. Silly as it was, I had to promise her that Mary would not hear and that if she did, she would never tell. With that assurance, Mary was welcomed grudgingly to the loft, and her pinch marks began to fade.

Sleep came more slowly to me after this change in our arrangements because thin as Mary was, her little body next to mine made my sleeping place almost too hot to bear. Some nights I welcomed this time for thinking, and I amused myself with games of remembering: the three most beautiful things I had ever seen, the liveliest song I had ever heard, the finest food, the longest story. Almost every one of those memories had my mother square in the middle of it, but some nights I could not picture her clearly, could barely remember the way she smiled. On those nights I sank very low in spirit and fell to thinking of the future, which brought me lower still. How was I ever to make connection again with Aunt Margaret? And how could I be sure that we were safe at Turtle Creek as I waited and hoped? Those were the nights my prayers came without prompting and with a fervor that would have made Sister Olive proud had she only known.

TWELVE

*T*n July of that year, when the passage of time had dulled my hopes and fears alike, there came a day when I was almost alone. Sister Olive had taken Abby and Lydia to the Elders' Family to help the Sisters with their work. A new house was being built for converts in the center of the village, and with the laborers called in from every corner of the Believers' land, there were extra men to feed. Only Liza stayed about our house. Her job was to mind the baby, a pairing that seemed to make them both content.

All the other girls, even Mary, had gone to the schoolhouse, for these hot weeks before harvest were the ones set aside for girls to have lessons with Sister Malinda. It worried me that Mary should spend so many hours within Darcy's reach. I knew that Sister Malinda had a reputation for firmness, but I did not know if she could contain one so sly as Darcy. It would have pleased me to be at school myself; a few other girls my age were there, but I had been dismissed before I started. Months before, in the short winter session not long after we came to the Shakers, I had been required to meet with Sister Malinda. I read every passage she set before me, and did all the ciphering, and wrote two verses of Scripture perfect to the letter. It startled her, I think, for she did not seem to know what to say. She smiled finally and shook her head and told me that my schooling was already complete, that my time would be better used elsewhere. It was a compliment, of course, but I regretted her decision. It was not just that being at the school would let me watch over Mary and bring some change of scene. I truly missed the times my mother and I had bent our heads together over a book or over my slate. There would surely still be some small thing for me to learn anew at the Shaker school, I thought.

Yet disappointed as I was to be denied the sight of words on a page, I was gratified on that day to be almost free, unburdened of small voices and the watching eyes of Lydia and Sister Olive. I remember that I sang to myself as I went about my work and that the tunes I chose were ones the Believers did not favor. I was singing as I rolled a crust for our supper tart when Liza peered in at me from the doorway. The baby was on her hip, and they both blinked at the dimness within.

"Susannah?" Liza's voice was hushed. "I do not know what I should do."

"What do you mean?" I said, and I noticed that her basket was almost empty. "Are there not berries enough for a tart?"

"There are heaps of berries." She put her basket on the doorstep and shifted the baby to her other hip. "It's not that. It's—there's a woman out on the path. Should I run to get Sister Olive?"

"What woman?" My voice threatened to catch in my throat. "Is it a Sister?"

"I do not think so," whispered Liza. "She lets her hair fall."

"What did she say to you?" I was trembling so that I had to grip the edge of the pastry crock to keep my fingers still.

"She asked me was William Arden's daughter still at this house."

I let my breath out slowly. "What did you say?"

"I said I could not tell her." Liza dropped her eyes. "I do not mean to be dull-witted, but I only know our own names, like Prudence and Abby and Betsy." She bit her lip. "Do you know who William Arden is?"

I did not say. My heart was pounding now, even as I wiped my hands on my apron. "Did she leave? Is she gone?"

"Not exactly." Liza cast a troubled glance over her shoulder. "She walks but slowly, and she keeps looking back."

"Well," I said carefully, "I will take care of this. I have had experience with strangers coming to the house." I willed myself to step slowly around the table, to move as though nothing had happened that was of concern to me. "It is not all that uncommon, Liza. There is no need even to mention it." I paused beside her to pat the baby's little fat back. "Why don't you see if this one will sleep now? I can help you with the berries later on."

Liza nodded and gave me one of her sweet, grateful smiles while I hastened out to find the woman I knew must be Mary's mam.

"Mistress Bay!" I called softly as I flew past our garden. "Sarah Bay! It is I, Susannah! Wait!" I saw the edge of her skirt swaying beyond the bushes at the end of our vegetables, a flash of blue where there should have been only green. "Mistress Bay!" I called again.

She stopped, turned, and then, as I ran, I could see her clearly. I had not known how the sight of her would bring such a rush of feeling. For just one eye blink I seemed to see my mother standing there, and so when she opened her hands in a gesture of welcome, I went straight into her arms and embraced her as if she were indeed my own kin. Then I was embarrassed to be so forward, and I stepped quickly away.

"I feared you would not come," I said. "I thought the Gatwood boy would not tell."

"That one is a great talker," she said with half a smile, and I saw lines in her face that I had not noticed in the spring. She patted my shoulder but peered beyond it. "Where is Mary? Is she still here? Is she well?" The longing in her voice sounded very plain to me.

"Mary is with the others," I said. "At the schoolhouse. She fares well, I think." I said nothing about Darcy and the pinchings.

"Has she changed? Grown taller?"

I shrugged. "She's a trifle taller, I suppose, but mostly the same." I shrugged again, for I was impatient to ask questions of my own.

A flicker of disappointment crossed the woman's face, and she dropped her eyes, as if the tall grass in which we stood were worthy of her attention. "Forgive me," she said after a moment. "I forget that you could not know what things a mother would hope to hear."

I wondered in that instant what my own mother would ask about me if she could. The pain of a year past rose up in my throat. "Oh," I said, "I think I do know." I took a breath. "Mary has learned all the letters in her name," I said, rushing on. "She is quiet but very quick. She sleeps beside me so none might tease her while I am not watching. And she wants to see you. Very much." I did not know that there were tears on my cheeks until I tasted them at the corner of my mouth.

Sarah Bay hid her face in her hands. "I am in anguish every hour Mary is gone from me," she whispered fiercely. "If she were here, I think I would flee with her this very day."

"Would the law not bring her back to her father?" I asked, for it was a question that needed an answer in my own life as well.

"Oh, yes," said Mary's mother, "if they found us."

"Well, then, they would find me if I went away to my aunt Margaret," I said with a sinking heart. It was not even a question. "My father would tell them where to look."

Mrs. Bay dabbed at her face with a corner of her apron. I did not know if she wiped away the damp heat of that afternoon or tried to stop tears of her own. "Mayhap they would not wish to go that far to find you," she said. "As for me, all my relations are close to this country. The child and I would need to be in hiding among them somewhere and take false names and depend on the silence of others to live out our lie. It is a great injustice," she said, and bitterness had replaced the longing in her voice. Her pale eyes glittered. "All that I want is to raise up my one and only child, to see her grow to womanhood and have a family of her own. Heaven knows I have tried and tried to find a way!"

My mother would have said just such a thing. I felt as close to Sarah Bay at that moment as I had to any other person since we came to the Shakers, but it was a connection born of such distress that I could not even speak of it. She seemed so distraught about her situation that I hesitated now to ask the questions that burned within me about my own.

"Ma'am," I began softly, and she brushed one hand across her eyes as if clearing cobwebs.

"I am sorry, child," she said. "It is you we must consider. I have messages. I tried to come before this, but this is a long, hot way, and my time is short." She smiled ruefully. "I have hired on at the inn, cooking for others to feed myself. It keeps me close by but much occupied, I am afraid. And you know I must creep around when I come here. I was so outspoken once that I am most unwelcome now."

I scarcely heard this, for my mind had fastened on the word *messages*.

"Please, ma'am," I said, "what can you tell me?" My aunt Margaret would have arranged something, I thought. She would have persuaded my father to let me go with her. She would have made Eldress Ruth listen to reason. On some unnamed day in these past weeks my aunt would have been thinking how much I favored my mother, and then she would have gone about mending my broken future. "What can you tell me?" I said again. I could scarcely wait to hear.

"I will give you Mrs. Wardwell's letter," Mary's mother said.

I must have shown my confusion.

"Your aunt Margaret Wardwell," she said. "We met and talked several times, and she brought me the letter just before she left."

"Left!" I cried. "Do you mean she has gone home? Without me?"

"Listen, now," said Sarah Bay, and her voice took a stern edge as she dipped down into the high grass and loosened one shoe, from which she handed up a limp little paper folded many times over. "Your aunt stayed as long as she could. Word came for the friend who brought her here that his father was taken very ill, and so she had to go back with him. A woman her age does not make such a trip without someone to look after her. But she tried everything while she was in the town to find a legal way to take you home with her."

"Gone!" I said slowly. I did not want to believe it.

"Hear me now," Mary's mother said. "Your aunt

105

was sorely disappointed to go without you. She left a good sum of money with Benjamin Gatwood and his wife, and the purpose of it is to pay your passage to Philadelphia as soon as you are free to go."

"That will be years!" I said, trying to steady my voice. "Years and years! I cannot leave here by my own choice until I am grown to adulthood. My poor aunt will be—" I did not finish.

"Never fret," said Sarah Bay. "And do not worry about your welcome in Philadelphia, Margaret or no Margaret. She has a large and lively household, so she says, with many cousins who will gladly make room for you."

I did take some momentary comfort in the notion of cousins, but there was no pleasure in the thought of the years I must yet spend among the Believers, stiff and straight and narrow in all my deeds and words.

"There is another thing, Susannah." Mary's mother clasped her hands together so tightly that patterns of pink and white appeared along her fingertips. "Mischief is still afoot for Turtle Creek. I know it will happen, and soon. I do not know how bad it might be. There are certain men who have complaints like mine against this place. They have talked of it to me, and I hear them ranting on with one another over their bread and ale. Their wives are gone, or their grandchildren, or their inheritance. A few of them came to the Shakers, like me, but could not in conscience accept all the beliefs that came to light. Some of them have little respect for the order of law and even less patience. A few of them are liars, and those are the ones who have spread stories about how the women are beaten and the children mistreated and kept in ignorance. They're trouble-makers, plain and simple."

My mouth was suddenly very dry. "What do you think they will do?"

"They are getting up a militia," she said, "and these armed men will march against the Shakers to—"

Here I shuddered, and Mary's mother hesitated.

"—to try to drive the settlement away from this territory, I suppose. They are circulating a regular subscription paper for men to sign up. Shameful is what it is, although heaven knows I would like to send the Old Believers back to the state of New York myself." She sighed. "If more reasonable men do not prevail, child, there will be a mob, and a mob is far worse than a militia. In a mob every man does just as he pleases."

My heart thumped. "Whichever should hap-pen," I said, "I will be afraid. What do you think I should do?"

"Please," she said, "whatever else you do, I beg of you, please take care of my Mary!"

"Yes, ma'am," I told her, although I could not think how I would protect even my own self from a mob of men with weapons.

"And then you should watch for me," she said. "When the danger comes here—if it looks bad—I will try my best to come for Mary. It's one thing to live with the knowledge that she is here when I think she is safe, but when I think of her in harm's way, I cannot endure it. I will take the both of you away if I can."

My breath caught for a moment in my throat. "Where can I watch for you?" I said. "How would you know where to find us?"

Sarah Bay let her hands rest on my shoulders. "How can I tell you what I do not know?" she said. "Pray this all comes to naught. But if there is trouble, watch the woodlot. I will try to come there. I think you are a sensible girl. You will know what to do."

She turned and walked away from me then without a word of good-bye, across the edge of the Gatwoods' precious cleared land toward the trees that concealed her coming and going. For a long time all I could do was stare after her.

THIRTEEN

I cannot say how long I stood at the edge of the field that day while my mind sorted the meaning of Sarah Bay's words. I tried to picture what a militia would be like, or a mob. I imagined a crowd of people and a great commotion and a sound like guns, a sound that grew so persistent and so real that at last I came to my senses and looked around me. To the west I saw that dark clouds had grown tall along the horizon and overspread the sun. The thunder was plain enough, although I could not yet see lightning. When I raised my hand to wipe away the sweat that trickled around the edges of my cap, I realized that I still held Aunt Margaret's letter. I bit my lip as I opened it, taking care not to pull the paper apart where it had been so tightly creased.

Dearest Susannah . . . I began to read in spite of the storm coming, in spite of Liza waiting at the house. I had no thought at all for the half-rolled pastry drying on Sister Olive's table or the sorry lot of berries in Liza's basket.

Now that I have seen you in the flesh, my aunt Margaret wrote, *I am more than ever determined*— That was as far as I could go, for just then I heard high voices on the rising breeze and looked up to see the figures of Sister Olive and all the girls of our household scurrying home with the weather at their backs. There was no place for me to hide.

"Susannah!" Lydia called to me.

"Hurry!" That was Mary, flinging out her arm as if she could gather me in and carry me along with her. "Storm's coming!" she cried.

I crumpled Aunt Margaret's letter in my hand and stooped quickly to force the wad of it into the top of my shoe before I ran, limping, to join them. I had to tell Sister Olive when she asked that I had walked out beyond the garden to see if they were coming ahead of the rain and that I had stepped on something that gave my ankle a little twist. It made me sorry to tell these lies, but Olive seemed to pay my words little mind. She was puffing along behind the others with a grim expression, and she did not even try to prevent Lydia and Abby from linking arms with me, strange as that was, nor from chattering as we hurried toward the house.

"Guess what we heard from the Sisters at the Elders' Family!" challenged Lydia. She was all aquiver. Her voice was just low enough to go unheard by the little girls, who were a short distance ahead of us and squealing in the first spatters of rain. The thought came to me that Sarah Bay would be wet to the skin; I hoped she would find shelter from the lightning and the wind.

"Guess!" Abby insisted, digging her elbow into my side.

"What?" I said shortly, for I felt little patience.

"Maybe I shan't tell you!" Lydia said, but of course she could not resist. "An army might come here," she confided, close to my ear.

"The Sisters could talk of nothing else," Abby said. "It might be soon."

"Is that not wicked?" Lydia demanded. "I think it is the most evil thing I ever heard!"

I took a deep breath. "Where is such evil in an army marching through?" I asked, baiting her, for I wanted to know more about what she had heard.

Lydia made a sound of disgust. "Not marching *through*," she said, "marching *to*. No one is certain of the purpose, but it proves how surely the world's people are against the Believers."

"The Sisters told us to pray and pray," Abby said,

"and to keep our faith and nothing would happen to us. Because Mother Ann had just such trials as these up in New England."

"And she endured." Lydia took up the story in my other ear. "I have prayed already," she said, "when the older Sisters were with us and we had to keep silence."

"I started to pray," Abby confessed, "but I kept worrying instead."

I squeezed Abby's arm in sympathy, but then we had to separate and run, for there was a single mighty crack as lightning and thunder came almost in unison.

"Run!" screeched Sister Olive. "Get in the house, all you girls!"

Jennet and Betsy cried in terror as the rain came pouring down, but we all had pushed inside by the time the hailstones began to fall. Some of the little girls had never seen ice in summer before; I had not seen it many times myself. The novelty of it helped calm their fears, and luckily the clatter of the storm passed quickly, leaving behind a slow and steady rain. Liza, celebrating our safe return, put the baby down long enough to dash outside with a crock in her arms and scoop up hailstones before they could melt. They were not much bigger than cherry pits. Mary helped her dole them out among us, so that we all had cool tongues there in Sister Olive's steamy little keeping room. For a moment it was a happy time, with much laughing and crunching and the pretense of shivering. Even Sister Olive smiled, once she had decided such a small hailstorm would not have hurt the garden. It was odd, I thought, that we should have such a rare moment of enjoyment just as our prospects began to look so bleak.

For my part, I let one of the larger bits of ice melt in my mouth as I folded my pastry into its pan. Then I cobbled together a filling from the few berries we had plus two handfuls of dried apples that I had tried to save as treats for Mary and Betsy. There were snap beans in the kettle, but not a great lot of them. My prayer at that moment was that no one should be too hungry for the evening meal and that there should be no complaints. I longed to escape to a place where I could rescue Margaret's letter from my shoe, ease the sore it was making against my foot, and settle down to read her message. Yet it was very late in the day before that came to pass.

Dearest Susannah . . . I read the greeting again in fading light, having escaped all prying eyes by volunteering to empty the slops from supper. It was Liza's turn for this chore, and I hoped she would see my eagerness to do it as an apology for leaving her stranded in the house for so long. None other of the girls was likely to follow me to the muddy little rubbish pit behind the thicket, not even Mary. Even so,

I lifted aside some wet branches and backed in among the leaves, concealing myself so well that I had to bring the letter very close to my nose in order to decipher the smudged lines of ink.

Now that I have seen you in the flesh, I am more than ever determined that you should have the life your mother would have wished for you, which is the life that she herself deserved. I pray that you will be able to come home soon so that you may enjoy the advantages of family ties and the refinements of a great city. To that end, I have left funds and a good lot of instructions for you in the care of Benjamin and Eunice Gatwood of Lebanon. They appear to be upstanding people who will help you along your way.

I hardly dared to breathe. It seemed as if all my future had been inscribed on this one bit of paper. Yet I knew that I must hurry; I made my eyes race as best they could along the page.

Mariah, your mother, was my favorite among all the nieces, very quick in her mind, fair of face, and clever at all manner of things. I expect you remember these good qualities in her and have begun to show them in your own person. Here I had to pause in my reading to blink away tears. How could I have forgotten any bit of my mother? I wondered. For at that moment she was so real to me, so clear, that I felt I might look up and find her watching me.

You should know, the letter continued, *that when I*

heard of her impending marriage to your father I was dismayed. Although I did not know him, I had known his family for two generations, and I considered many of his people to be lacking in judgment as well as the finer graces.

These words took me much by surprise. My father had never spoken of his own family to me, except to point out the names of his parents in the Bible he had taken to be his constant companion after my mother died.

My doubts were confirmed, Aunt Margaret wrote, when, not long after your birth, he announced his plan to take you both away into the wilderness of Kentucky. My late husband and I joined your grandparents, God rest their souls, in trying to convince him of the folly of this course of action. Your mother very nearly refused to go with him because of my persuasions, and this so angered your father that he forbade her ever to write to me or ever to speak of me again. This much I know from the one letter she sent in defiance of him. She wrote that she could not bear to have me think she had grown distant by choice. She assured me that she loved him, and she hoped that the wide sweep of a new territory would help him conquer the melancholy thoughts that bedeviled him.

I thought how I had lived with my father all my life, save for these past months, and I hardly knew him. I had not reckoned before that knowing anything about him could be much concern of mine. By his actions he had taught me that silence and distance were the natural order of things between father and daughter.

I cannot agree with your father's decisions, Aunt Margaret's letter went on, *but I choose to believe that whatever the spiritual life he has taken for himself, he might still listen to rational argument regarding your upbringing. I will continue to consult with my lawyers and to correspond with the leaders of the Shaker settlement in the hope of arranging a timely release for you.*

My heart hammered as if I had run a great distance, but the truth was that I feared I would never go anywhere, despite my Aunt Margaret's petitions.

Be hopeful, Susannah, she wrote in tiny, spidery script at the bottom of the page. *Put your trust in the Lord. Remember that He cares for everyone, not only those who make special claim to the name of Believer.*

With abiding affection, your great-aunt, Margaret Wardwell.

Twice more I read this letter, to commit every word to memory. It buoyed my spirit even as it puzzled me, this new look at the family I called my own. I should have liked to carry the page with me and take it out from time to time for reflection and for assurance that I belonged to someone, even if that someone was very far away and very old. Still, I did not know how I could safely hide this paper and, if it should be discovered, how I could explain it away.

With shaking hands I tore the letter once and twice again and then in tiny bits, which I scattered in the rubbish pit and covered with wet leaves. Then I brushed the dampness off my clothes as well as I could and went into the house in time for prayers.

FOURTEEN

The little girls were not supposed to know about the trouble that was coming to Turtle Creek that summer, but they did. Mary was the first to grasp the meaning of our whispers and the looks we taller ones exchanged above the heads of the others. Like as not, she had heard us murmuring that first night in the loft. Our words were softly spoken then but not chosen with care, for we all thought she was asleep.

Lydia raised herself on one elbow and, speaking low, told Liza that an army was coming, was marching against the Shakers. "Pray!" she directed. "We all must call on the Spirit and Mother Ann to protect us. The Sisters at the Elders' Family said we should."

"There might be shooting and clubbing and what

all!" Abby put in. Her voice held more excitement than fright, but the words made me shudder.

Liza groaned faintly in the dark. "I haven't learned to be good enough yet to meet the Maker," she whispered. "I haven't had time to get to be a real Believer."

I could not be silent any longer. "Liza," I said, "you mustn't worry. The Lord cares for everyone, not just those who call themselves Believers." I was grateful that my aunt had given me these words; they were some comfort to me in the gloom of the loft.

"Susannah!" Lydia's whisper was full of reproof. "You have no call to give advice in spiritual matters! That's for me to do. Sister Olive almost as much as said so. Remember? It was the day that Liza and the others came."

I could feel my cheeks flame. "Here is something for you to remember!" I hissed back at her. "Think of the times when Sister Olive's family have come to warn us of danger." I imagined Lydia recalling her meetings with Joseph Gatwood and her color flaring brighter than my own. "Think how no one paid them any heed," I said. "Where were your prayers then, Lydia?"

Silence held for one long moment. Then it was Abby who spoke. "I did not believe those people," she said.

Lydia made a low sound in her throat. "Small wonder no one believed them." Her voice shook only a little. "They took their story from that woman."

"What woman?" Liza whispered.

"Mary's mother," Abby said.

"She is wicked, Liza," Lydia said. "An apostate."

"What? Poss-what?" Liza's voice trembled.

"Apostate," Lydia repeated. "She came here and claimed to be a Believer, but then she denied the faith and left. It's shameful, like being a traitor."

"I would never leave," Liza said earnestly. "I like it here."

I had to hold my lips tight together to keep my thoughts from escaping aloud. I wondered if Mary's mother had ever embraced this faith at all. Her sojourn at Turtle Creek had been more than likely her husband's doing, I thought, just as mine was my father's. While I could not say that outright, it was too hard to be silent.

"Maybe Mary's mother would know more about the plans of the world's people than we could ourselves," I said. "I, for one, believed what the Gatwoods came to tell us."

"You would," said Lydia in a tone I did not like.

Abby muffled a giggle, and just then the little one beside me stirred on her blanket.

"Shhh!" I said. "Mary might hear us." We fell

silent after that, although sleep was a long time coming, at least for me.

In the days that followed, Mary stuck to me the way a little green burr clings to a stocking. She asked questions that she had not asked before: "Where does my mam sleep now? Why does she not come to see me anymore?"

I longed to tell her how much her mother cared for her and wanted to be with her but I dared not. If Mary should report that I had said any word at all about her mam, there would be questions from Sister Olive, I was sure. And I could not afford questions or the consequences that would surely follow. "Watch for me," Sarah Bay had said, and so I felt that I must manage to stay with Mary at the Gatwood house, where I might watch the woodlot, for there was some chance, some trifling chance, that Mary's mother could free the both of us from the Shaker yoke. Thus I was silent with Mary about this most important thing even though as the days wore on she grew more fretful and harder to console.

I do not know if it was Mary who whispered to the other little girls the secrets she had heard in the loft or if, more likely, Abby had been the one to tell them. I knew that they had heard something when one day as they were at play in the moments between their chores, I saw them marching with sticks held to their shoulders like guns. It was Darcy who seemed to be in charge, with Jennet and Prudence in her troop. Betsy marched without a stick, and the others jostled her. She was their prisoner, I supposed. Mary hung back alongside the house, talking softly to a twig-baby in a game of her own. After a moment or two of watching I turned back to my own occupation in the garden, disquieted but convinced there was no real harm in their game.

It was late summer then, and the music of insects rose and fell around me in a chorus of tiny songs that my mother had taught me to admire. I turned to thinking of her, wondering what she would have done to prepare for our coming trouble. Always before I had thought I knew what she would say or do or think, and so I still could have her guidance, be her daughter, though she was gone from me. But that day I realized I could not even imagine my mother facing a militia nor the prospect of one. Of a sudden I felt so alone, so bereft, that I could have laid myself right down among the vegetables and wept—and I might have done so had I not heard at that same moment a terrible shriek.

I leaped to my feet and ran toward the house, letting the cabbages I had gathered fly out of my apron. Mary was backed against the wall, white-faced, as Prudence and the sisters poked their sticks hard against her ribs. It was Betsy who was shrieking, and when she took a breath, I could hear Jennet and Prudence taunting Mary: "Wicked Shaker!" "Go away!" "Take her to the woods to live with the snakes!"

Sister Olive reached the little girls before I did and launched into such a scolding as would blister their ears. She took the offending sticks and snapped them over her knee without missing a word. It pained me that she included all five, as if Mary and Betsy were part of the game instead of its victims. When I thought she had finished, I rushed in to claim those two, one with each arm.

"I will take Betsy and Mary to help me in the garden, Sister," I said, and although she glared at me, I hurried them off to the shelter of the bean rows where I could wipe their wet faces and calm them. Betsy went off soon enough to find Liza and the baby, but Mary and I stayed for a little time, hidden and cool.

"Prudence does not like me," Mary said with her nose buried against my side.

I could not deny it, but I made soothing sounds and rubbed my fingertips around and around in the small of her back.

"Jennet is mean to me," she whispered. "Very."

"I know." I patted her. "And does Darcy still pinch?"

"Sometimes." She paused and turned her face up

to me. "And my mam is never coming back. I know it." Her shoulders began to shake against me in silent, heaving sobs.

There was no strength left in me for secrets. "Oh, Mary, no," I said softly, sitting down and pulling her into my lap. "Your mam wants to be with you again. And she will try to come soon. She told me so herself."

Mary sat up straighter and drew a quivering breath. "Did you see her, Susannah?"

"I did." I smiled and wiped her cheeks with the hem of my apron. "She wanted to know all about you, and I told her you had learned some of your letters."

"Did she like that?" A little light came alive in Mary's eyes.

I nodded. "She was very proud."

Mary scrambled to her feet. "Where is she?"

"Shhh!" I warned, keeping firm hold of her skirt as I got up beside her. "Your mam is not here now, and we cannot tell anyone she has been here or that she is coming back. It has to be our secret—promise me!—and we have to be patient."

The little face grew sober again. "When will it be?" she asked.

"I—I cannot say." I remembered then that this comfort I had held out to Mary would come to her only when there was danger. "She—she did not know when she would be able to come, but she holds you close in her heart. She thinks of you every day. She said that to me."

Mary sighed. I held out my hand to her, and we went to gather the cabbages I had dropped.

"Remember not to tell," I reminded her once, and she nodded.

On our way to the house we met Lydia coming to tell us that Sister Olive had taken to her bed with a throbbing head. I was to come in at once and mix up a remedy for her while Lydia and Abby gave the little girls their hoecake and milk and walked with them to their lessons.

It was my turn to sigh, for I would have kept Mary with me that day if I could. Instead, I spent the afternoon in the dim of the house, bending over Sister Olive's Bible to read out Gospel passages at her direction. She claimed these would do her more good than the brew of herbs and willow bark I gave her to drink, although she showed little interest in the familiar words as I read.

"Are you feeling better, Sister Olive?" I inquired when I paused to freshen the damp cloth I was using to soothe her forehead.

Her eyes squinted at me from the edge of the well-worn linen. "I will say this for you," she said. "You have Shaker hands. I doubt many girls can cook and tend a garden and work with powders the way you do. You have good, useful hands."

I flushed with unexpected pleasure. Sister Olive seldom gave praise to anyone, least of all to me.

"What you still need," she said, "is the Shaker spirit to go with them. I've yet to see one sign that you have turned your heart to God."

My flush deepened. "But—" I began to protest, and then held my tongue. What could Sister Olive know of my own true heart except that it did not keep quite the same rhythm as her own?

"The Believers' way is so simple," she said, and I stifled a sigh, for I had not asked for instruction. "You are very stubborn or you would see it for yourself. What you have to do, child, is put away all your attachments to the world. People or possessions, one is as bad as the other. For union in the Spirit, you have to be separate from the world. Surely you've heard the Elders explain it. But you, now, you wear your ties to the world as plain as the ones on your apron."

I made a face that Sister Olive could not see. "'Love ye one another,'" I quoted firmly. "It says that right in the Scripture. And all the stories in the Bible have families in them, or almost. Even Mary, the mother of Jesus, had a husband!"

"Impudent girl!" Sister Olive said. Her voice was not so much angry as it was thick, like the voices of my father's friends in Kentucky when their waistcoats smelled of whiskey. "You know better," Olive said slowly. "Mother Ann has moved us on. When you have separated yourself from connections of the flesh, then you can yourself be godly. Do you not want that, child?"

In truth I did not. I wanted to be as human as I could be, a joyful soul like my mother before me. That seemed plain and right, but I thought mayhap my feelings were no more intelligible to Sister Olive than hers were to me. I made myself busy turning the cloth on her forehead, and the only answer I gave her was that she should try to sleep.

"And obedience," Sister Olive went on, although she no longer seemed to be talking to me. "That is the thing. Perfect obedience to God and Mother Ann. And Elders and Eldresses among us to pass on the rules that keep us from straying. Do everything in order, by the rules. But with children . . . so hard . . ."

"Sister Olive?" I touched her shoulder, for it seemed to me she was no longer herself.

"So weary . . ." Now she whispered, and her eyelids drooped. "Such wicked trouble. Too much . . . More than an old woman can stand. All these girls . . ." For a moment I was alarmed, but then her eyes went shut, and her mouth fell open a finger's width, and out came Sister Olive's familiar snore.

Relief washed over me, for sleep meant that she would be all right even though my medicine had been too strong. I watched her for a moment as she breathed noisily in and out. If I went away, I thought—*when* I went away—I might never see Olive again. What moved me then I do not know, but I lifted the cloth from her forehead. "Poor Olive," I whispered, and touched my lips quickly to her brow.

After that I went out into the garden to find two good squashes for our supper, as she had instructed me early in the day. I picked beans instead, and such a small rebellion cheered me as usual, but only a bit. In my deepest heart it worried me that Sister Olive had shown so much distress. I wondered if she was troubled by all the same things that troubled me or if there was something else, something I was not yet clever enough to dread, bringing turmoil to her mind.

FIFTEEN

No one needs to wind God's clockwork, my mother always said. That week went on and ended, and the Sabbath came as usual. I remember odd things about that day's Meeting. My father looked straight at me, that was one thing, but I did not know what to make of it. There were not so many visitors that day, hardly any women at all, and not one face that was familiar to me. Some of the strangers wore fine clothes and sober countenances; others swaggered and threatened on the walk outside the Meeting House. It was not hard to believe that some of them meant harm to someone.

I cannot recall the tunes we sang that day, nor do I think I took any pleasure at all in the dancing. I might as well have been stamping my feet at Sister Olive's doorway to rid my shoes of garden mud. The speaking went on a long time so as to include not only our regular exhortation in the faith but also cautions about the new trials that would likely come to us. We were advised all to go about our regular business should any of the world's people come to menace the village at Turtle Creek.

"Mark this day," said the Brother who spoke at that service. "It is the year of our Lord eighteen and ten, the month of August, the twenty-sixth day. This day we prepare for a new test of the strength of our belief." I did not welcome his affirmation of trouble to come. The very prospect brought a sour taste to my throat, for all that I thought it might bring Sarah Bay and a chance to move on from this place. Still, I took some pleasure in his words. Imperfect though memory always proves to be, I do not recall that it was the custom of that time to speak the day's date at Meeting. Nor was there in Sister Olive's house any calendar or almanac; we spoke less of dates than of seasons and of the days of the week that marked our progress from one Sabbath to the next.

Hearing the number of that day set my mind adrift. It was more than a year now that my mother was gone, soon to be a year since my father and I had set out for Turtle Creek. Before the twenty-sixth day of another month I would pass into my fifteenth year. What would another year bring me? I thought about my old aunt and her long journey, and I wondered, as I had so many times that week, what exactly she had meant by "the refinements of a great city." And then I thought about my mother and how close she once had been to Aunt Margaret, and so I stole a glance at my father. His straight back told me nothing.

I remember how glad I was when that worship was over. We saw a doe and fawn together at the edge of the woodlot on our way back to the Gatwood house, and I was sorry that Mary was not along to see them. None of the little girls was with us that day; they were at home with Liza to look after them. That meant Sister Olive had feared for their safety, I thought.

I was sure of it from the way she prayed over them when we began our afternoon confessional.

"Watch over these little lambs, O Lord," she said, and she moved down the row of them, touching each one's head in turn. I saw Prudence squirm away from Sister Olive's wrinkled hand. We were out under the apple tree, which made barely enough shade for the lot of us, but there was a good breeze to keep us comfortable. The sunlight falling through the leaves made a pretty pattern on all the girls' little caps, and I smiled to think that not even the Elders could disapprove of such godly ornament. If I had closed my eyes properly in prayer, as Lydia often reminded me to do, I would not have seen these things.

And because my eyes were open, I was the first to see two men striding up the path alongside our garden.

"Oh!" I said aloud in the midst of Sister Olive's supplications. My heart feared to beat until I was able to see that it was two Brothers who approached us, not eager fellows running ahead of a mob. Under the apple tree no one else spoke, although my small outburst drew glares from Sister Olive and from Lydia. All of us watched the men come closer. I did not know the older one, and I did not recognize the other until Mary moved. At first she stepped toward him, and then she came to me and hid behind my skirt.

With barely a glance at Mary, he came quite close to Sister Olive and inclined his head. "I am Brother Thomas Bay," he said, speaking low, but not too low for us to hear. We were all well practiced at listening. I could not keep myself from staring at him, for I had not known his face well. He was older than his wife, I thought, and not as well featured. His expression was grave but not unkind.

Sister Olive nodded to him without speaking. Maybe it was that she did not know a rule for talking to a Brother who appeared in the middle of the Sabbath, without warning.

"The Elders agreed that I might come to see to it that my natural daughter is still here and safe among you," he said.

"See for yourself," said Olive, pointing to the part of Mary that was visible at my side.

The man's eyes flickered in our direction. "The reason for my concern," he said, turning his attention back to Sister Olive, "is that I feared her mother might have taken her away."

"We know of that danger," Sister Olive told him. "Someone is always with her. Usually that one." She pointed again in my direction.

He did not even look. "My wife was seen nearby," he said, "just a few days past. I think it is certain she was trying to make some contact."

I prayed that he would not turn to me and ask if I had seen her. Within the folds of my skirt I fumbled for Mary's hand and squeezed gently, hoping she would remember that what I had told her was meant to be secret. The child breathed in and out as if she had a sickness, but no words came.

"Be more wary of the woman now," said Thomas Bay as his silent companion nodded for emphasis. "I have been told she has taken on as cook at the Sign of the Golden Lamb, where she can hear all manner of plotting against us." His voice dropped so that it was just above a whisper. "It would not surprise me to find she has joined it, she is that bitter."

I clenched my teeth against the words that came to my tongue, the protests, the arguments. Any sound I made would be one sound too many.

"We will turn her out soon enough if she comes here," Sister Olive promised him. She scrubbed one hand across her forehead, as if it might again be aching. "I would sooner keep this child in the house forever than let that backslider have so much as one look at her face!"

All under the apple tree, girls shifted their weight and took here and there an uneasy breath. Mary was stiff as a stick at my side.

Thomas Bay took half a step backward. "I ask only that you be wary and keep this child that I have brought to God among the faithful," he said. "As for the woman, you should pray for her. Ask the Lord to open her eyes that she might believe."

And what if she *does* believe? I cried silently. The face of Mary's mam transposed itself in my mind and became that of my own mother. What if she is godly in her own way, and it is just not the way of the Believers? Why should anyone think less of her for that?

It was not until Mary tugged her hand away from mine that I realized my fingers had tightened painfully around hers. This small movement drew her father's attention, and he turned to look at us. His expression showed great feeling, but I was not sure what name to give it.

"Grow in the grace of God," he said finally, and then the Brother who was with him placed a hand on his shoulder, and the two of them turned and walked away.

For a few fragile moments there was nothing to hear except everyday sounds: birdsong and the hum of insects and the faint scolding of squirrels. Lydia was the first to find her voice.

"Well-l . . ." she said slowly, turning to look at me and drawing out of that one word and that one look an entire accusation.

Abby's mouth flew open, but it was Liza who spoke first.

"Susannah!" she cried happily, as if she had made a great discovery and offered now to share it with me. "Maybe that was the woman you talked to on the day of the storm. You know, the one you sent away."

Mary began to cry against my skirt. My mouth tasted of metal.

"Come here!" Sister Olive said to me, and although her voice was quiet, its tone was ominous. Her face had turned a purplish red clear to the edge of her cap.

I took a few steps toward her, but awkwardly, for Mary clung to my leg.

"You have lied to me," Sister Olive said.

"No," I said, taking a breath. "It was just that there did not seem to be anything I needed to tell."

"Silence is its own lie," she said angrily, and her hands came up, shaking. For a moment I thought she intended to strike me.

"Did you speak to . . . that woman?" she asked.

I nodded.

"And not the first time, either," Lydia said.

"Why was she here?" Olive demanded.

"She asked about Mary, Sister Olive," I said, trying to steady my voice. I worried that if Olive grew one whit more agitated, her heart might burst right there under the apple tree. "She asked questions that any mother might ask," I said.

"And was one of them about where she might find this child to carry her away?"

While I considered how to answer, Darcy and Jennet began to whisper and fuss until finally the smaller one came to pull at my skirt. "Did our mother come, too?" she said. And then Betsy, who had been trying to pat Mary's shoulder, began to cry along with her in a thin wail that was most aggravating to hear.

"Quiet!" Sister Olive shouted. "All of you be quiet! You are too much of a care!" She glared at us all, even Lydia. "Get on your knees to God," she said. "You pray while I think what to do."

I was grateful for the soft earth beneath the apple

tree that cushioned our knees and for the many creatures in the grass that gave entertainment to downcast eyes, for Sister Olive was a long time thinking and praying to herself. Then she came to stand over us and pray aloud with a fervor that woke the baby, who had just gone to sleep with one hand wrapped in the hem of Liza's skirt.

When Sister Olive gave us leave to stand on legs made shaky with so much kneeling, it was clear that she had come to some decision. She did not tell us what punishment there was to be or if it was to be mine alone. The others treated me to baleful silence as we went in to make our evening meal. I feared I would see no more friendly faces in Olive Gatwood's house, save for Mary's. Even the baby cried when I tried to pick her up. I remember how I felt then, empty and wretched.

I lay wakeful on my blanket that night, thinking of what had been and dreading what might be. Mary had been summoned to sleep at the side of Sister Olive's bed. Somewhere, I thought, at that very moment, men might be polishing their guns and making ready to march against Turtle Creek. My aunt Margaret was gone far away. I could not yet see how things might come to be worse.

SIXTEEN

When I woke that next morning, I thought for a moment that I was home in Kentucky, with my mother singing over the kettle as she began her day's chores. A great bubble of happiness welled up inside me. Gradually then the feeling slipped away, as dreams do, and bit by ragged bit the real world returned to me. The voice I heard was Sister Olive's, and the hour was very early. The light that showed through the cracks in the wall of the house was dull and gray.

Olive's singing was rough and flat to the tone. *"In yonder valley there grows sweet Un-i-on,"* she sang. *"Let us ARISE and drink our fill."* It was so odd to hear Sister Olive's hymn before breakfast, and so unpleasant, that I scrambled up and into my dayclothes and was down the ladder before the others began to stir.

"Make yourself busy," she said without any greeting. "We have more than we can do this morning."

She did not seem to be angry with me, and that was a wonder, I thought. "Shall I go out and fill the wash kettle?" I asked. It was Monday after all, and wash water took a long time to boil.

"No time," she said. "No washing today. Get a cloth out of that basket and see if you can wrap those jars tight so things won't spill out along the way."

"What do you mean?" I said. "Along what way?"

"We are all going into the town," she said.

I caught my breath. "To stay?" I could not think of any other reason for taking our larder with us.

"We should be with the others," Sister Olive said. I could see her face in the growing light, and it showed satisfaction in every line. "I have been considering this for a while," she said. "If any great force comes, we will be safer all together."

"No, Sister," I said, fighting back the panic that threatened to close my throat. "What would an army care about just the few of us here? But they will go for sure to the Elders."

"Tut!" she said to me, clattering all our cooking spoons into a single pile. "May God sweeten your tongue. I am not fooled. You have made some plan with that Bay woman. What other tie would make you want to stay here?"

She stopped her work long enough to watch my face go pale.

"I thought as much," she said. "If we are here, I'll worry about every shadow I see, thinking it's that woman come for her child. And I'll not be able to trust you anymore at all to look after her."

"Please, Sister Olive," I whispered. "Please let us just keep on here. There is not so much to be afraid of. Remember those men outside the Meeting House yesterday? If they come back, they will not come looking for us. They will go straight to the center of things."

She frowned briefly. "No matter," she said. "I have tried everything I know to make Believers of you all. It's time that someone else took on your instruction."

"Please," I breathed. But of course it was useless to beg.

The little girls were all aflutter when they heard we were leaving, even though it meant half the usual breakfast and twice as many chores. Abby squealed when she heard the news, and Lydia beamed. Her good humor included even me. She chattered and laughed as we shook out our blankets and bundled them around our Sabbath dresses, neatly folded.

"I cannot believe how wicked you have been and how well it has turned out," Lydia said cheerfully. I knew she had been longing to be with the Sisters, for she had confessed it to me as a sin of discontent. "The Sisters do everything just so," she went on. "I've seen them. When they do the Brothers' mending, they fold every finished piece alike."

Abby nodded. "And after they scrub their pots and kettles, every one goes back in the very same spot in their cupboard."

Lydia beamed. "Once I was there when they had a meal, and they all sat down together at the exact same time. The Sisters know how to do everything the right way."

Exactly alike seemed a boring plan to me. I remembered my mother with her own mending and how she would say, "Look, Susannah. Most people turn the seam this way, but here is how I do it."

I scowled. "Likely the Sisters will not have room for us," I said, "except in the Children's Family. Or the barn."

Abby and Lydia scowled in return, but I knew that Sister Olive could not have made arrangements for our coming, and I did wonder how we would be received. Decisions in Turtle Creek were made by Elders and Eldresses, I thought, not by ordinary Believers.

The sun had climbed halfway toward noon that

day when Olive Gatwood shooed us all out of her house and closed the door after us. We were loaded with bundles and baskets and jars that made us slow. I took some of Mary's things to lighten her load, and I kept watch on her even though she had to walk beside Olive. Darcy had already been after her that morning, tweaking and teasing.

It was not so long a way to the Elders' Family dwelling and the Meeting House and the Children's Family beyond, but that day it seemed the most arduous of journeys. The weight on my back was naught compared to the one in my heart. When we walked alongside the garden, I thought what a refuge it had been for me and what regret it brought me to leave it. I stumbled often as we followed the track through the edge of the woodlot, for my inclination was to study every tree and every bush, wondering if it could conceal Mary's mam. There was no hope that I might watch for her to come to the woodlot now; the buildings at Turtle Creek were too far away and sheltered too many eyes that might observe my coming and going.

When we passed the great barn, Mary made her way to me and whispered about the horses and cows she had seen there. All I could do was nod, for I found it painful to remember the dark of that night. And then, of a sudden, our line of sight to the Elders' Family was clear, and every one of us, I think, halted and took in a long breath at the same time.

A crowd of the world's people was in the town, milling about on the roadway and leaning on the picket fences that enclosed the most prominent buildings. I did not see an army, but I saw one man with a bullwhip and several with clubs.

"Should we not go back?" Liza said, and her voice squeaked on the last word.

I could see the throbbing of Sister Olive's pulse in one blue line near her temple. She cleared her throat. "The Lord watches after his own," she said. "Step along after me."

Some of the men hooted and jeered and made rude noises as we picked our way among them.

"What pretty little packhorses!" one shouted, but two others offered to carry our things for us.

"Keep your eyes down!" Sister Olive directed. "And pray! Pray as never before!"

I took many extra gulps of air on that walk, but I could not resist looking around me, and that was how I noted some of the strangers were disputing with others, begging them to put weapons away.

"All right, Judge, all right," I heard one man say to another as they both moved away from us. "You know me for a decent man. I ain't about to hurt a child."

In spite of the turmoil, no one bothered us after we went in the women's gate at the Elders' Family.

Olive led us on the path to the kitchen entrance and called through the open doorway for Eldress Ruth. After a time one of the older Sisters came out and asked our business, but her jaw dropped further with each word of Olive's answer.

"Dear Sister," the woman said, "you could not have picked a poorer day." Then she took Olive inside and left us all standing there with our bundles beside us. There were a few Sisters in the Elders' garden, which covered a huge expanse, and a few more at work over their own washing near a shed some distance behind the house. Now and again they peered around their bonnets at the men in the street, but for the most part they went on about their business.

In our own little group we shuffled about and whispered, ill at ease.

"Was that an army?" Darcy asked, pointing back the way we had come.

Abby laughed. "No, silly," she said. "Armies have guns." But Abby's voice was higher than usual, and her cheeks pinker.

I kept Mary so close beside me that I could feel the shivers passing through her body, one after the other. "Keep watch for your mam," I whispered very close to her ear. "Tell me if you see her." Perhaps Sarah Bay had been in the woodlot after all, I thought, and I had just missed her. I had a wild hope that she would be in the very next wagon that rattled into the town and that Mary and I would ride away with her while the Shakers were too busy with their intruders to pursue us. Yet I felt certain that Mrs. Bay would not come back into the midst of the Believers unless she knew Mary to be there. And of course it was the Gatwood house where she expected Mary to be. There was no chance, I thought, for Mary or for me. If Mary's mam came for her, came for both of us, she would not find us. I looked at my feet so that no one might see the torment in my eyes.

Presently a young woman came out of the house with a jug of water for us to share and a good many sweet cakes done up in a cloth.

"Sit you down here and rest, little Sisters," she said, and held out her arms for the baby. I wondered by the ease of her movements if she had once had a child of her own. "I hope there is a way to get you settled soon," she said, "but everyone is busy planning what to do when the marchers come. Even Eldress Ruth is troubled today."

Lydia had been mumbling to herself—prayers for deliverance, I thought—ever since we had gone by the Elders' barn. Now she stopped. "When are they coming?"

The young Sister shook her head sadly. "Today," she said. "Within the hour, I expect. We hear that militiamen have been gathering at Captain Kilbreath's, hundreds of them, maybe as many as a thousand. And just look at all the crowd that's already here!"

I watched Lydia's face lose every bit of its color, and that one time I understood her feelings. A thousand men! The very idea of it brought a sick feeling to my stomach.

"Do you know why they want to come here?" Lydia asked her. "Will they—" She could not go any further.

"They say they are coming to take Colonel Smith's grandchildren," the Sister said, "and I don't know how many others. I've heard all sorts of things."

My body felt hot and then cold. Could I be one of the others? Could Mary? Was it possible that this horde of men, frightening as it was, might bring me some good?

The Sister shook her head again. "But you shouldn't worry," she said. "No children are going to be taken anywhere this day. There are plenty of authorities here to help settle things, even Judge Dunlavy himself."

She talked on, but I listened no longer. I kept quiet and attended to the tiny spark of hope that had been kindled within me.

Finally Eldress Ruth appeared and sent us to the

schoolhouse to wait out the trouble. Sister Olive stayed behind—to meditate, Lydia said, although she knew no more about it than the rest of us. The young Sister who had talked to us took the baby inside and did not bring her out again, to Liza's great distress.

Two of the Brethren waited for us at the fence, and after we had deposited our bundles inside the door, as directed, they escorted us down the road toward the school. It was noisy and crowded in the middle of the town, with so many men and horses gathered, and the animals were making such mess underfoot that it was hard to walk. I picked Mary off the ground and carried her, while Abby did the same with Betsy. They were our two smallest and the most likely to be trampled by unwary feet. It did not seem likely that men with hatchets and knives and pitchforks would watch where they stepped.

"Close your eyes," I whispered against Mary's bonnet. "You need not look at this."

"No," she said, and she tightened her arms around my neck. "I will not see the horses if I close my eyes. Or my mam."

"Oh, Mary—" I regretted that I had asked her to keep watch, and I could not decide what to say to her. "We are not sure she will come today," I said at last. "There are only men here, as far as I can see." That was not entirely true, for I had seen many

147

speckles of color appearing at the near edge of the woodlot, and I suspected that women had come there to see what would happen to their relations at Turtle Creek, be they Believers or intruders. Perhaps Sarah Bay was among them by now, but she might as well have been in Philadelphia with my aunt Margaret for all the chance we had of reaching her that day.

Just then a shout rose up all around us, with such a surge of bodies that we girls had to stop and cling together.

"Go away!" Prudence spit over and over toward the men that surrounded us, as if she were shooing chickens off a doorstoop. "Go on away! Get!" None of the gathering acknowledged her, for they had not the least interest in our little band. They had all begun to move toward the north road, and I could not at first see why. But then through the crowd I caught a glimpse of men on horseback, row after row, riding into the town. My eye went first to their military hats and uniforms and then to the swords and gun barrels that seemed to twinkle in the afternoon light. I had never seen such a spectacle nor been so full of dread. What lunacy of mine, I thought, to have considered the possibility of help from such a gathering. I think my mind would have given over to panic at that moment had I not been able to see, here and there, plain ordinary men struggling to keep the peace. There was even one figure who seemed to scold the mob in the familiar voice of Benjamin Gatwood, but he moved away so quickly that I could not tell for sure.

The Brethren begged us to hurry. Truth to tell, I believe they were more mindful of their own safety than of ours, for some of the men threatened them as they passed. My own father came into my mind then, and I wondered where he was and if he would be safe. But there was no time to heed that worry; it took all my attention just to step from one clear spot to another without losing my companions. Mary seemed to gain in weight as we went along, and she clung to me so tight I could scarcely breathe. She would not go to Liza, who offered to take her. The other little ones fussed and whimpered, and who could blame them? It was only Lydia who seemed to take strength from the occasion. I had expected her to go into one of her swoons and fall into disaster, but she put away her earlier fearfulness to walk in the lead and call back to us with words she thought to be encouraging.

"Remember Mother Ann!" Lydia reminded us again and again, but that was no encouragement to me. She was not the mother I wanted to remember.

I said my own prayers that day and thought my own thoughts and rejoiced when we came, un-harmed, to the school.

SEVENTEEN

I have heard many accounts of what happened between the Believers and the world's people at Turtle Creek that day. I was there, and yet all I can tell of it is my own part, the thing that happened while we were in the schoolhouse, shut away.

I do not remember if it was a day when regular lessons were scheduled, but the school was crowded with children, boys and girls alike. Both the teachers were there, Sister Malinda for the girls and Brother John for the boys, as well as the helpers that each of them had. There was much coming and going in the road outside, and now and then a Brother or Sister would slip in quietly to see if this child or that was safe and secure. It was no wonder that the pupils fidgeted and stared at the windows rather than their slates.

Lydia and Abby and Liza and I huddled awkwardly at the back of the room. Lydia busied herself in prayer, although she had to be silent in deference to the teachers. Liza watched Sister Malinda so closely that I realized she might never have had any lessons of her own. Abby fussed with her bonnet strings and twitched at every new sound. It was very strange, I thought, to have no tasks, no way to occupy our hands. I would even have been glad for spinning, the worst of chores, the one I tried always to avoid. That day I would have welcomed anything to slow my racing thoughts.

We waited for what seemed hours, yet the shadows had lengthened only a fraction when messengers came from the Elders' Family to collect Brother John and Sister Malinda and those of their helpers who could be spared. There was a committee from the militia, they said, who had met with one of the Elders and two other Believers to present a list of demands. Now all of the leading people among the faithful must meet and consider an answer. I tried hard to hear every word that was said, but there was too much soft scuffling in that schoolroom, too many sighs. Perhaps the Believers would be convinced to release Colonel Smith's grandchildren after all, I thought. And perhaps someone had spoken, too, on my behalf, and on Mary's. I wanted so much to know that I opened my mouth to question one of the messengers, but then I thought better of it.

After a flurry of whispers too low to hear, Sister Malinda and one helper put on their bonnets and filed out past us while Brother John and two of his helpers and the Brethren from the Elders' Family went out the other door. That left two Brothers and two Sisters in the school with us all. I did not know the name of the Sister who took the lead, but I was grateful when she asked me to be a helper with the little girls. The time passed some faster after that, and it pleased me that Mary ventured a smile when I stopped at her bench to hear all the row recite their letters.

"J, K, L," I had to prompt, and "P, Q, R." I squatted on my heels so that I might put my face near their faces. Thus was I concealed among the benches of children when a commotion arose at the men's door. I did not look up at first, but then my mouth stopped shaping letters, for I heard a familiar voice, quite loud.

"Where is she? Is she not here?"

It was my father, much distraught and disheveled. I stood, but he did not see me then as he continued to speak to the Brother who was helping with the boys.

"She is not at Gatwood's place. No one is. I went

to see if any harm had come to them, but—"

I waved my hand at him, for it would have been rude to speak out, and yet I wanted him to know I was there. All the children were staring.

"—all of them were gone," he went on. "Food-stuffs and bedclothes and all. I came running back to report they had been stolen away, but then someone told me the children had all come here."

He scanned the room again, and saw me, and whatever words were next on his tongue floated away.

"Susannah," he said, and expelled a great breath. "I thought you had . . . come to harm."

"We all are safe," I said quietly, moving toward him, "for now."

He looked at me in such a peculiar way that it was all I could do to return his gaze, and when he came to meet me in the middle of the room, he reached for my hand and held it. There was frowning all around us at such unseemly conduct, but I did not care. The tie between parent and child should be stronger, I thought, than any rules the Shakers could make about separation. And yet my father's gesture took me by surprise. It had never been his way to show affection, least of all to display it by touch, in view of others. It came to me that something might be amiss with him, that he might have something grave to tell me. I could feel myself begin to tremble as the Brothers and Sisters came toward us, so that we were gathered, the six of us, between the two ranks of children, boys and girls.

"Daughter," my father said to me, "I want you to know that you have my leave to go. If you choose to live with Margaret, I will not prevent you from going away with her."

I know a sound escaped my lips and that all eyes were on me, but I was too much astonished to speak. Why could he not have said this weeks before, I thought, when I might indeed have gone away with her? But surely he must love me, for now that he had seen the danger, he wanted me to be in a safer place. I beamed at him. I could not help it.

"But I hope you will not go," he said quickly. "I pray you will not."

My smile gave way to confusion. "But—" I said, and could not continue.

He swallowed before he went on. "I want you to be here and embrace the life of the Believers because it is the holy way," he said. "But I have wrestled with my soul, and I have come to see that I can no longer require you to stay." He dropped my hand and used both of his to gesture to the group.

"All of you are witness to this confession," my father said. "I told this child she could not leave the care of the Believers. But I gave this direction for unworthy reasons. It was not so much that I cared for her spirit as for my own selfish pleasure. I wanted to keep her among us so that I could see her, because I counted her my own child and I was too weak to give up the whole of my ties in the flesh. And," he said, "and . . . the worst of it is that I desired to be reminded through her of the feeling I had for her mother when all that must be behind me."

He was only a step away, but his voice came to me from what seemed a great distance. "What I must do is release you, Susannah, but I pray that your feet will be guided along the right path."

By then my eyes were wet with tears. How could my father possibly regret that I reminded him of my mother? What a hateful notion that was to me, and yet—still—I could not but rejoice, for he had set me free. Even as I wept, I wanted to shout and sing. I could make my way to Aunt Margaret, and no one might stop me. All I needed was some kindhearted soul to take me to Lebanon, where I could get help from Benjamin Gatwood and his wife. My thoughts had raced before; now they flew. I scarcely heard the remonstrances of the Brothers as they pulled my father away to speak to him or the solemn advice the Sisters offered me. I hardly noticed how the children shifted in their seats as they strained to watch and hear us, and I paid no mind at all to Liza and Abby and Lydia, who stared at me with their mouths open.

Free! I thought. I was smiling again. I could be free!

I do not know how long it took me to realize that something was not quite right. I sensed that in my amazement I had forgotten some important thing, and I squeezed my eyes tight, trying to think of it. When I opened them again, I found that I was staring across the rows of children and full into Mary's face. Betrayal was written there as clearly as if it had been inscribed on her slate. Her eyes were round and unblinking, although the tracks of tears showed on her dusty cheeks. The elation I felt began to slip away. How could I leave poor Mary? I thought.

"I beg your pardon, Sister," I said to the one in charge. "That little one over there—Mary—the one who came in with me, she is crying. I would comfort her if you will allow it." The Sister furrowed her brow but nodded. As she walked back to her place to restore the order of the lessons, I made my way between the benches to Mary and knelt in front of her.

"A, B, C, D, E," rose in a chorus all around us. Mary did not say a word, but she reached for the hand I rested on the bench beside her. Her fingernails bit a row of tiny half-moons into the flesh of my wrist.

"Mary, listen," I whispered. "There are others here to take care of you." I pointed toward Liza and the others at the back, but I knew as I spoke that my words were hollow. "Some of the girls at the Children's Family will be kind," I said. "Celia will be there, and Jane."

She looked down at her lap, hiding the effort it took to swallow her sobs.

"Your mother would come for you if she could, Mary," I said. My lips were tight against the child's cap, that I might speak for her ear alone. "Your father says you must stay. That was only yesterday. You heard him." It grieved me to see her misery and to feel it, for her breathing heaved in and out against my own body as I leaned close.

I searched for some hopeful word that I could say to her, but none came to me. Darcy and her sister were glaring at us, I realized, as they stumbled through their letters. A little shudder ran along my spine as I thought of the mischief that could be done to Mary when I was not there. I thought how small Mary was, and how needful. And how dear she had become to me.

Yet, I thought, a way had finally opened for me to leave this place. I could almost feel the kiss with which my aunt Margaret would surely welcome me, could almost hear the words of greeting from cousins yet unknown, could almost see that life which my mother had deserved and which waited now for me.

Just then there was a new burst of shouting outside and a brief clatter of horses. I looked from Mary to the window and back again. Philadelphia was far away, part of a story that my mother had not told me. I felt all at once that it was foolish to belabor the future when we all might still perish at the hands of a mob that very afternoon. It seemed as if my own hopes took leave of me then, and I was empty of everything but the needs of the moment.

Mary lifted her face and looked at me. "I want my mam," she said, and every word echoed within me as if I had spoken it myself.

"Shush, little one," I told her, for I knew well enough what comfort she needed to hear. "I will stay and watch after you, Mary," I whispered. "I will be your mam."

When I think of the rest of that fateful afternoon, it is hard to know what is memory and what was pieced together afterward. I do remember that I moved and spoke and came to smile as usual, and that I refused Lydia when she demanded to know who Margaret was. It may have been that my demeanor was normal, yet my spirit was as lifeless and wooden as one of Mary's twig-babies. I remember that I recited my way through innumerable alphabets with row after row of little girls. Eventually, when the afternoon was late and at its hottest, a whole troop of the world's people came in with Brother Matthew Houston and some others of the Believers.

"Show these people our Testaments," Brother Matthew said to the teachers. "Someone has lied to them, saying our children are ignorant and not allowed to read Scripture for themselves."

Several small Testaments were produced, and a boy with a crooked nose was called on to read from one of them. Then two of the girls were chosen to display their penmanship, and one to recite her letters. After that, a boy did sums as fast as the visitors could call out numbers.

"I see no fault in any of this," a man in a fine suit said with some disgust. He proposed that everyone should go home and leave the Shakers in peace.

But others wanted to question us. Did we have enough to eat? "Plenty! Plenty!" the children's shout went up. Were we mistreated in any way? A whole chorus of "No! Never!" came in answer. Was there any reason we should need the help of an outsider? These words made me ache, although perhaps it was my own silence that caused the pain. I was not the only silent one, I noted, but some, like Lydia, made such an eager denial that it must have appeared we all were speaking.

When the questions were done, our visitors commended the children for their schoolwork and their good behavior. Then they left, and all the threat was gone out of them. The few militiamen among them seemed almost embarrassed.

In a while we heard the clatter of horses as the troopers took their leave of Turtle Creek. Then by twos and threes and more their supporters left, and also the observers and those who had defended the Believers. There had been much talk, we learned later, many charges brought and answered, and new threats made. Yet at the end of that day, which began in fear, the mob simply unraveled, leaving the village untidy but unharmed. The Believers had endured, had not agreed to leave their land, had not given up one absent wife or handed over a single child. The question of Colonel Smith's grandchildren had been put in the hands of the authorities. We were all accounted for. And I was still among the Shakers, holding tight to Mary's hand.

EIGHTEEN

*W*e lived after that in the Children's Family, Mary and I and the others, and I tried for a time to be a Believer in my heart. I stopped my ears against the memory of my mother's voice and strained to hear instead the tune to which my father danced. Once at Meeting I did fall into a swoon, and brief though it was, it sent Lydia off into a fit of jealousy. Still, in the end I could not be convinced that God meant for any of us to keep to ourselves as the Shakers wanted or to live by their rules, which seemed to grow more complicated by the week. Sister Olive Gatwood's house, I realized, had been cozy and homelike in comparison, and I came to miss Olive herself as well as the small freedoms she had allowed me.

I might have been happier if Mary had flourished or if I had been more able to keep my promise of watching over her. The tasks I was assigned, mostly spinning, kept me often away from her. I tried to find a moment to be alone with her every day; but after one of the Sisters chided me for having a special favorite, I had to be devious even to say good-night. Mary grew more and more silent, more watchful. I knew that she was still waiting for her mam, still hoping. It was a hard thing to see.

The heat of that summer passed, and autumn came. Nights grew cool. All the woods took on fiery colors, and most days the air was crisp and bright. One day when clouds moved in and I was sent to see to our washing that hung behind the house, I heard the sound of a wagon and then several voices at the front. Loudest of all was one of the Sisters.

"Begone!" Her voice thundered with such power that I could not mistake a syllable. "All these children are under our protection. They have no need of contact with the world outside."

I forgot the washing and made my way to the corner of the house, trying to see without being seen.

"It makes no matter," the Sister was saying. "She may have had permission to leave, but you see that she did not."

I raised my hand to my mouth lest some sound give me away.

"You are not to disturb her peace with any messages now," the Sister said. "All she needs to know is here."

It was all I could do to keep from revealing myself, for it was certain that I was the object of their conversation. If there was news for me, I wanted it. Anger began to overtake my judgment. I took a huge breath in preparation for bursting around the corner of the house and demanding my message in person.

I had taken no more than one step when I saw a little way off the unmistakable lanky form of Joseph Gatwood. Abruptly I halted. It was clear that he was not then visible to the Sister, for he gestured wildly to get my attention and then spoke to me with his hands in motions I could remember but not understand.

"Go home, my friends," I heard the Sister say. "You tend to your business, and we will take care of ours. And be sure to take your boy!" Joseph disappeared, and I heard his grandfather's voice and the rattle of their wagon going away, although I could not see it.

I leaned against the house then, for I thought my legs might fail me. For weeks I had not allowed myself to think how much feeling still was in me, what longing I had to hear of Sarah Bay and my aunt Margaret and even Sister Olive's family. I almost could not bear the thought that I was missing some word from one of them, or that Joseph Gatwood had tried to tell me something and I did not know what it was.

The rain must have begun some time before I noticed it, because I did not save much of the wash from being wet all over again, and that only with help from other girls who came rushing out from their tasks inside. My slowness earned a strong rebuke, which bothered me only a little. But Mary heard it, and it made Mary cry, and that did not please the Sisters, either. I was weary unto my soul of the Children's Family, of all of Turtle Creek. I wondered why it was that the Shaker way could bring comfort to my father and such grief to me. Perhaps, I thought, it was just that I was still counted as a child and he was grown.

That night I dreamed of my mother, a dream that woke me long before daylight. I did not remember the dream itself, just the pleasure of having it. I lay listening to the quiet that is left behind when rain stops, thinking for a moment of nothing. Then there popped into my mind, with inexplicable exactness, the meaning of the message that Joseph Gatwood had shaped with his hands. The first motion was for reading, then folding, then chopping, and after that a circle that took both his arms to make, followed by a jab to the center of that space. It meant there was a letter, folded, at the woodpile, and I would find it in the huge old stump where we split kindling wood, tucked into the crack that ran across its center. Joseph must have hidden it, I thought, while his grandparents confronted the Sister, or perhaps even before. The Gatwoods had delivered my message after all.

I was up in a minute and into my clothes, creeping with my shoes in my hand past the room where the Sisters slept and then downstairs. I felt my way along to the kitchen, testing every step in the dark with a careful toe, and then I found the door and slipped into my shoes and was outside. The clouds were breaking up and drifting away, letting a little moonlight peek down on the shed behind the house and on the woodpile beyond. I could see just enough to stay out of the worst of the mud as I hurried to the stump and probed the split in its middle with eager fingers.

Confident as I was of finding a letter there, I had not reckoned how wet a piece of paper would be after it had spent so long in the rain. It was a poor, slippery thing that I pulled from the stump just as the moon broke free of the last of the clouds. By dim silver light I saw that I had once had a message, but I had it no longer. The paper was stuck to itself, the ink smeared. There was not one word that could be read.

I think there is no word for what I felt that night, for the mix of anger and despair and loneliness that left me too heavy to move from the stump, too weary and hopeless to cry. I sat for some time there—it was long enough that I began to feel the chill—and then somehow my mother came to me. I do not mean that she was there. I saw no wraith in the moonlight. But I felt her presence. I remembered her then in all my senses and in my spirit, and resolve began to grow in me. I was still her daughter, and I would do what I could to live as I thought she would have counseled me. For a moment I bowed my head to speak my gratitude for this guidance and to ask for strength. And then I moved to take my leave of the Shakers.

It is a wonder to me when I think of that night, how I was able to do what I had not done before, how many troubles and pitfalls there might have been but were not. It was some miracle just to go back into the house undiscovered and bunch the blanket on my narrow bed as if I were still in it. Then I made my way among the sleeping children to Mary's bed, woke her to silence, found her clothes, and carried her down into the kitchen. There I dressed her, gown and skirts over her nightshift for warmth, and helped her with her shoes. She submitted without a whimper. I found our shawls on the rows of pegs near the door; they were quite new, and although it seemed like theft, I thought we needed to take them.

The moon was a blessing to us, giving Mary the courage to walk on her own feet and letting me be sure of the way. The town of Lebanon was but a few miles distant; that much I knew. And I recognized which road we must take to get there although I had never traveled it. From the beginning I thought it best to walk alongside, even if that meant scrambling over obstacles and soaking our shoes in the long wet grass. The road itself was soft with mud and showed every track laid through it. We must not leave our shoeprints there for the Believers to follow, for follow they would, just as I watched now for the ruts made by the Gatwoods' wagon wheels.

"Are we going to see my mam?" Mary asked once of me when we were far from Turtle Creek.

"I hope so," I said.

"Will there be bears?"

"Not one," I said, although I was not quite so sure as I made myself sound. The road had skirted the woods for much of the way, but I did not know how many stands of trees might lie ahead.

"But I would like a bear," Mary said, and I laughed, surprising myself. It had been some long time since I had laughed.

"A bear would like you," I said, "for breakfast." That made her giggle, but I was suddenly regretful that I had not thought to borrow some provisions from the Children's Family larder. My stomach was growling, the moon was fading in dawn's first light, and I was unimaginably tired.

NINETEEN

$\mathcal{B}$y the time we reached the edge of the town, I had Mary on my hip and was only plodding, step after weary step. There were many wagon ruts in the roadway now, and I had no hope of knowing which one might lead to Benjamin Gatwood's stable. Two dogs had already barked at us, and though I had not seen any human face, I could not be sure that no one had seen ours. I stood for a moment, considering. When the Believers roused themselves and all the children for early chores, two empty beds would be discovered, an alarm would be sounded, and a search would be on. The Sister who had confronted the Gatwoods yesterday would think of them immediately, and some of the Brethren would be on their way to

Lebanon, were perhaps on their way even now, traveling on horseback, galloping where we had crawled.

"Come, Mary," I said, sighing. "We need to rest for a while." Close as I thought we were to welcoming arms, we must delay. I found us a thicket far from the road and well away from any house, and we hid there. When I was satisfied it sheltered no snakes or unfriendly creatures, we curled into our shawls to wait. Mary slept, but I did not mean to, for I wanted to see who from among the Believers might go by. Then I thought to close my eyes for just a minute, and when I did, my body followed its own command, and I, too, slept.

The sun was well overhead when we started on our way again. Although I had straightened us both as best I could, brushed away some of the mud splatters and wrung out our wet hems, I feared that we looked scarcely presentable. We had left our caps and bonnets with the Shakers so that our hair hung free, tangled though it was. I did not wish to think what lies I should have to tell if someone tried to question us, but I hoped that from a distance we might pass for sisters on an errand.

We walked only a little way before we came into the town, and then I could not decide whether we should walk fast or slow to attract as little notice as possible. There was a fair number of people about, and we brushed quite close to a woman with a large basket. She turned around for a second look at us.

"Beg pardon," I mumbled, and hurried us along, trying to think what we should do next.

Mary was gawking at horses in the street and at all the sights around her. "Look, Susannah!" she said. "Those buildings have letters painted on the front."

"Don't stare so," I told her, smiling. "People will think we do not belong here." In truth I, too, was searching with my eyes, looking for some clue to the whereabouts of those we had come to see.

"Look!" Mary said again, pointing at a large building made of logs. "Look at that sheep!"

My eyes followed her finger, and I rejoiced. What she had spied was the sign of the Golden Lamb, hanging over the tavern door. I grabbed her hand and pulled her around the building toward the back, where we found an entrance door ajar and the tantalizing aromas of soup and bread in the air.

"Knock, Mary!" I said. "Stand up tall and bang on the door."

"Am I supposed to ask for food?" she said, hanging back.

"Just knock!" I said, hoping I had not made a mistake.

She did it because I told her, without expectation of any good thing to come. And then the door opened to reveal the face of Mistress Sarah Bay, frowning at such an interruption to her work. They both gasped at once, mother and child, and cried out and reached for each other. Then they both wept, and I had to weep with them, although I had as happy a heart at that moment as I had ever had. Mary's mother stretched her arm to me and brought me tight into the little circle that she and Mary made, whispering thanks against my shoulder.

"Oh, just to see her!" she whispered. "What a marvel! God bless you!"

But Mary's mam did not spend long exclaiming over us. Instead, she gave us each a slab of bread and a wedge of cheese and sent us straightaway on to the Gatwoods. She repeated the directions twice, saying the Brethren had come to her earlier that day to look for Mary and to put others on watch. We would be safer with the Gatwoods, she thought, until she could join us and plan what else to do.

"Take good care," she said, looking over Mary's head to make sure there was no one in the lane behind the tavern. "And hurry! It will be better if no one sees you long enough to think twice about it."

It took some effort to disentangle Mary from her mother's skirt, but once we got started, it was simple enough to find the house where Benjamin and Eunice Gatwood lived. It would have been judged far too ostentatious for Turtle Creek, I noted. We crept to their back stoop as Mrs. Bay had told us to do, and knocked, and waited a moment that seemed to last for hours. Then the door creaked and came open, and we practically fell into a keeping room that smelled of herbs and spices. Something about it made me think at once of home.

"Dear girl!" Eunice Gatwood embraced me as warmly as if I were a long-lost granddaughter. "And Mary!" She bent and put a kiss on Mary's forehead. "Mr. Gatwood will be so glad you are here," she said, patting the both of us as if to reassure herself that we were real. "He's out making inquiries just now. When those Shakers came this morning, we thought you might really be lost. I am much relieved to see you."

What I remember then is comfort: a padded rocking chair, hot cider in a cup, ginger cakes. Silent Mary found her tongue and chattered happily in answer to all of Eunice Gatwood's questions. When Mr. Gatwood came in, she greeted him without prompting.

Benjamin Gatwood beamed at her and rested one hand atop her head before turning a serious face to me. "We offer you our condolences, Susannah," he said.

I was startled out of the haze of pleasure into which I had settled. "What—"

"Did you not find your letter?" asked Mrs. Gatwood gently.

"I found it," I said, "but I could not read it. The rain made it too wet to decipher."

"Oh, child," she said. "I am sorry. Your aunt Margaret went to her Maker some weeks past, God rest her soul."

I could not speak. It was not surprise I felt, for I had thought much about my great-aunt's age. But it was a wrenching thing to lose my Margaret. She must have had great love for my mother, I thought, or perhaps even for me, to try so hard to bring me aid. Perhaps she was simply a person of great Christian charity, helping an unfortunate relative, but I had felt a strong tie to her. I had clung to the hope she offered me, and now I was not sure what I should do next. I put one hand to my face to hide the tears.

"The letter was from one of your cousins in Philadelphia," Mr. Gatwood said to my silence. "He sent it to us along with word of Mrs. Wardwell's death. He wrote us that he was inviting you to come join his household whenever you were able, and he implored us to see that the message reached you."

I managed a smile to show that I understood and was grateful, but I knew from the first moment that the attraction of Philadelphia was gone. No cousin's household would be the same as the one I had tried to imagine. Both of the Gatwoods talked on about their fondness for my aunt. During her weeks in Lebanon she had visited them often and told them much about her late husband and their children and their many travels, stories they repeated now for me and from which I took comfort.

By the time Sarah Bay came knocking at the Gatwoods' back door, I was beyond the first shock of the news about Aunt Margaret's passing. Still, I welcomed the distraction of greetings and Mrs. Gatwood's offer of tea all around, for I needed time to sort my thoughts before I spoke any word about it.

"I told them at the tavern I was feeling ill," said Mary's mother. She sat on a cushioned stool by the fire and pulled Mary down into her lap.

"Are you sick, Mam?" Mary patted her mother's cheek.

"No, no." She smiled down at her daughter. "I am hearty as I can be, absolutely blooming—because you are here with me." She began to run her long, thin fingers through Mary's tousled hair, and her face was grave when she looked at us over the child's head, mouthing words without sound: "Any minute now I fear they will come and take her away."

Mrs. Gatwood frowned. "Mary," she said sweetly, "come into the front room with me and help me look for the rag-doll my girls used to hold."

When Mary was gone, Sarah begged Mr. Gatwood to help her find a plan. "What chance do I have of keeping this child?" she said. "Or even of seeing her again?" She twisted her hands together with such force I thought she would hurt herself.

"It will not matter where I try to hide her. The Shakers will come for her and take her back because her father wants to have her there, and you know that the law will uphold his rights as a father. Judge Dunlavy tells me all the children are fed well and not mistreated," she said. "As if there are no other needs of consequence! He says I should learn to accept what must be."

Benjamin Gatwood sighed and tried to comfort her although it appeared he had no better advice to offer than the judge.

"It's hopeless," Mary's mother said at last into her hands.

In spite of my silence, I had been intent on every word. I could not bear the thought of Mary being parted from her mother now, again. And I worried for my own sake as well. "Can the Shakers come and take me back to my father, too?" I asked them.

Mr. Gatwood shook his head. "The story that came to us says your father gave you permission to leave, and in front of witnesses."

I nodded. "He did. But he thought I would go to Aunt Margaret. What if he changes his mind now?"

"It might come to a lawsuit, I suppose," Mr. Gatwood answered, "but I can't think your father would win it. And at any rate," he said, "you will be far away, out of reach."

I smiled. "No!" I said, and I went to sit on the

floor by Sarah Bay. "It is you and Mary who should be far away, out of reach," I said, touching her hand. "If I might be safe here, you can take the money that my aunt Margaret left for me and fly so far no one will find you."

"Susannah!" she protested. "What low sort do you think I am, that I would spend the inheritance of someone else's child?"

"But I want you to!" I said. "My cousins may be kind, but I feel no tie to them. I have no need to go to Philadelphia." Then the arguments began in earnest, with Mrs. Gatwood coming to join in while Mary cradled the rag-baby on a bench under the window. Was there any chance that my father would summon me back to him? they wondered. What would my cousins think if I did not accept their hospitality? What would become of me? What would my Aunt Margaret have wanted me to do? I cannot remember all that was said. What I remember is how the hunger grew in Sarah Bay's eyes as she came to see the possibility of my plan.

"My mother would want me to do this," I told them finally, and I had to make the words slow, for they were hard to say. "She would understand how a girl and her mother want to be together, ought to be together, if they can. And she would see that I am doing this to ease my own heart as well as yours."

"Come with us then," Mary's mother said, and for a moment I was tempted, but only for that one moment. Two could travel with less trouble than three, I thought. Besides, I was possessed of a strong feeling that I should stay.

In the end, Sarah Bay refused to take the whole of Aunt Margaret's money. She agreed with the Gatwoods that a part of it must be held back for me, for a dowry, if nothing else, they said. That suggestion pleased me. Shaker girls had no need of a dowry; having one reminded me that I was back again among the world's people.

There was a great flurry of activity then, so that Mary and her mother could slip away before evening fell. It was late in the season to start a long journey, Mr. Gatwood said, and late in the day, but every hour increased the likelihood that Brethren would come again to Lebanon, looking for Mary. Mrs. Gatwood put on her shawl and went out into the afternoon, to fetch a neighbor with a team and wagon. He winked at Mary and told her he just happened to be setting out to visit his brother in Cincinnati that very afternoon.

Mr. Gatwood spread a blanket from his stable in the wagon bed. "Use that to cover yourselves, you and Mary," he advised Mrs. Bay. "It won't be comfortable, but you both need to stay out of sight these first few miles. And don't forget the name of the man you should ask for to book passage upriver, and . . ." He went on and on with his instructions.

I held Mary while the neighbor ate ginger cakes

and Mrs. Gatwood packed one basket with food and another with assorted provisions for travelers. Finally there was nothing left to do, no plans left to make.

I hugged Mary until she squirmed. "I hope you see a lot of horses," I whispered, "and hardly any bears." She kissed me, and for a moment I thought she would cling to my skirt and refuse to go, but then her mother smiled encouragement at her, and she went happily to the wagon.

"Good-bye, dear girl," Sarah Bay said to me, and I was nearly overcome with feeling. When my own mother left me, she was too weak to say a word.

"Good-bye, Mam," I whispered now to Mary's mother. "Godspeed." Then she, too, was gone, and I had to remind myself that this was my own wish and it had been granted.

I stared after the wagon long past the time when there was anything to see, thinking of all the loved ones and the chances I had lost in a year's time. I was not sure where I would lay my head that night or whether my father would someday try to take me back to the Believers. In spite of all that, I felt my heart growing lighter. After all, I was my mother's daughter, free in spirit and equal to adversity. For the moment I was content, just knowing that she would have been proud of me.

EPILOGUE

*T*he Gatwoods took me in and gave me a family as well as a home. I cooked for them and made poultices for their rheumatism and did their mending, and between times I read every book on the shelf in their front room. I also became Mr. Gatwood's scribe as his eyesight worsened, learning much thereby about the mill he owned with one of his sons.

The Gatwood granddaughters became my bosom companions. We took turns quilting together on one another's patchwork so that we all could be notable housewives one day. We faced tragedy together. There was a disaster of nature in the year 18 and 11, when the earth shook and toppled rocks and knocked over a half-built barn in the countryside, injuring one of the cousins. After that came war, although it was a little one as wars go, with an uprising of the Indian nation close by. Still, we were young and found much laughter to share, and the faces we wore home from church were serene.

Joseph Gatwood and the other grandsons were like brothers to me, tormentors and protectors by turn, and finally trusted advisers. I made an appeal to them when it was time for me to think of marriage, and they spoke plain to me about which young men should come courting and which I should avoid. In due time Eunice Gatwood's nephew Abner Trumbull became my husband. A finer man never lived, I think.

Our children, and their children after them, have often begged me for stories. Their favorites are from my days among the Shakers, and their questions take always the same tone: Why didn't you go far away with Mary and her mother when you had the chance? I have never had a good answer for that, although perhaps it came down to something as simple as not wanting to abandon my father completely, whether he cared for me or not. He was, after all, my father, and he lived out his days among the Believers. Never once did he try to make me go back to them.

The settlement at Turtle Creek came to be called Union Village, and when I was grown, I visited there from time to time just to catch a glimpse of my father at Meeting or to offer a sociable word, which he would sometimes return and sometimes not. I think that his mind grew more troubled as time went on and that it was good for him to be safe among the Shakers.

The village changed over the years. It grew rapidly larger at first and then slowed in its growth so that it was not always waiting to gobble the fields of nearby landowners. The population settled also, into a pattern of mostly grown people and orphans. Once the ways of the Shakers were common knowledge, fewer families joined whole, to be broken apart. Union Village became a model for agriculture and purveyor of the finest seeds in all of our part of the state; I sent Mr. Trumbull there for garden stock myself. All these things made the Shakers better people in the eyes of their neighbors. The countryside relaxed its vigilance, and what had once been regular violence against the Believers became no more than occasional pranks. These were good, decent people, my friends and relations said, although they were more than a little eccentric.

We have traveled through that Shaker town, my family and I, hundreds of times since I left it as a girl. Each time again I think of the others I knew there. Some stayed and grew old as Believers, like sweet Liza, and Abby, and round little Celia. Poor Sister

Olive Gatwood fell prey to a stroke the year of the earthquake. I was never able to find out what happened to Darcy and her sister or to Prudence, although I inquired about them many times. As for Lydia, she left the Believers when she was old enough to do so and spent a year in Lebanon with her uncle's family. She set her cap for a number of unmarried men in the town, and among them was Joseph Gatwood. He was clever enough to discourage her, praise be, thus sparing me many tedious moments at family gatherings.

When I cross the Shaker land, it is always Mary who is uppermost in my mind, of course, Mary and her mother. Beyond the neighbor's report of their safe arrival at Cincinnati, we heard nothing of them for years, concerned as Sarah was about concealing their whereabouts. Then we had one letter full of love and gratitude, assuring us they were well and happy but giving still no hint of where they were. After that, nothing. I pray for them both to this day, although I do not know whether to count them among the angels or with those of us who toil on earth.

These days, when my carriage takes me into Union Village and alongside the present Children's Family dwelling, I admire the building itself. It would be hard to imagine a sturdier structure or a tidier yard. Or more obedient children, for that matter. The Shakers have acquired a fine reputation now for their care of orphans, and it is said they are kindly to the little ones. Then I remember that Mary and I were obedient children, too, and I look at the house again and wonder what longing might still be hidden there, what child cries itself to sleep wanting a mother's touch. I shudder to be reminded how much children are at the mercy of the grown people in their lives, how much they must bend to their parents' whims and intentions, for good or ill.

My own mother comes always to mind then, and I think how she taught me by example to love God and all His creation and how earnestly I have tried to leave the same legacy. I was a happy child and then for a time a lonely, anxious one, but all told, my life has brought me great contentment. I nod to the young Shakers when I pass, and I smile, and this is what I think: Be hopeful, children. Be hopeful.

AUTHOR'S NOTE

*T*he Shaker sect was founded in England by Mother Ann Lee, who came to America in 1774 with a small band of followers. By the time Shaker missionaries from the eastern United States made the difficult trek to Ohio in 1805, several well-organized Shaker communities were thriving in New England. But Ohio was still a frontier state. In order to build communities in the West (Ohio, Kentucky, and Indiana), the Shakers had to start from scratch. It took years for the western settlements to reach the level of spiritual refinement and simple comforts that the Old Believers had enjoyed in the East.

New Shaker communities were often in conflict with their neighbors. One of the issues was propriety.

Shaker dancing in the early 1800s was much less restrained than that of later years, and this activity—practiced as a form of worship—fueled many rumors that the celibate Believers were guilty of sexual misconduct. Property ownership was another problem area, as the Shakers acquired sizable shares of land to support their growing numbers of converts. Legal as these transactions may have been, settlers who had preceded the Shakers often resented this narrowing of the resources available for the community at large.

One of the sharpest conflicts between the Shakers and their neighbors involved questions of child custody. The matter was clear enough when orphans were taken in by the Shakers or when a parent placed children in their care in the hope of providing stability and a good education. However, when families disagreed among themselves about joining or staying with the Shakers, children were sometimes caught in a tug-of-war between a parent on the inside and other family members on the outside.

Custody disputes like these were among the issues at stake when hundreds of armed men marched against the Shakers near Lebanon, Ohio, on August 27, 1810. At that time several grandparents demanded the right to see their grandchildren or to take them away, but the Shakers argued successfully in every case that they were only carrying out the wishes of the parent in charge. (Hard as it is to believe, that day of confrontation ended with no significant injury on either side.)

If information about young people of the past were as easy to find as accounts of governors and generals, this book might have been about some of the real children whose fate was in question. As it is, Susannah and Mary and all the characters central to this story are invented. The details of their day-to-day life at a time when the community was just forming are speculative to a degree but anchored by fact where fact was available. For instance, the "world's people" did poison a horse in one of the Shaker barns in April 1810. There are occasional appearances by real people as well, like Eldress Ruth Farrington and Judge Dunlavy.

There were Believers at Union Village until 1912, when the few who remained sold the land and left the state. Unlike some historic Shaker towns in other parts of the country, this one has not been restored and opened to the public. The local Shaker legacy is kept alive in documents and artifacts at the Warren County Historical Society in Lebanon and at the Golden Lamb, where meals and rooms can still be had.